JUSTICE BEFORE LAW

JUSTICE BEFORE LAW

PAIN AND AGONY™ BOOK ONE

MICHAEL ANDERLE

DISRUPTIVE IMAGINATION

Copyright © 2021 LMBPN Publishing
Cover Art by Jake @ J Caleb Design
http://jcalebdesign.com / jcalebdesign@gmail.com
Cover copyright © LMBPN Publishing
A Michael Anderle Production

LMBPN Publishing
PMB 196, 2540 South Maryland Pkwy
Las Vegas, NV 89109

Version 1.01, September 2021
ebook ISBN: 978-1-68500-463-7
Print ISBN: 978-1-68500-464-4

THE JUSTICE BEFORE LAW TEAM

Thanks to the Beta Readers
Larry Omans, Kelly O'Donnell, Rachel Beckford, Mary Morris,
Kit Mitchell, John Ashmore

Thanks to the JIT Readers

Deb Mader
Wendy L Bonell
Diane L. Smith
Angel LaVey
Jackey Hankard-Brodie
Zacc Pelter
James Caplan
Peter Manis
Dave Hicks
Paul Westman

If I've missed anyone, please let me know!

Editor
The Skyhunter Editing Team

DEDICATION

To Family, Friends and
Those Who Love
to Read.
May We All Enjoy Grace
to Live the Life We Are
Called.

— Michael

CHAPTER ONE

If he had the choice, he preferred to play Go over Chess. There was something calming in the simplicity of black and white discs being moved around the board in a game that could take days to play. Both games required the players to think more than twelve moves ahead but no one played Go with a timer. When he had been on assignments with his former partner, a game of mental chess could take days to complete.

Now? Speed Chess took all the fun out of it for him, but the game did help to keep his mind nimble as he worked mentally through the Scotch Opening and the moves that followed.

Surveillance was tedious work, especially if you were six-foot-four and had to sit for hours and your eyes constantly had to switch from one hi-def lens to the other as your earpiece picked up every snippet of conversation.

He risked a couple of minutes to do some reverse chin-ups from a bar he had hung in the loft apartment while his shotgun mic picked up all conversations coming from the building across the street.

Talk about banality. He counted his fifty off and returned to his cameras.

The Sicilians and their Cosa Nostra had books and movies about them. Although he thought the term "organized crime" gave them too much credit, at least they had dipped their fingers into every available pool of vice accommodation.

On the other hand, the Camorra—not that he was judging anyone—had developed a singular focus. That was drug-running in partnership with their friends in the South American continent.

Pain, first initial M, had more respect for a gang that chose diversity than he did for one with such a limited scope of focus as the Camorra had.

The assignment he was on now was not official in any way, shape, or form. It was simply something he had to do. He didn't know if he had been listed as AWOL or MIA, but he was very sure that he was currently persona non grata with the officials. Nonetheless, he had no qualms about the limited focus he had chosen to take. Boredom was part of the process so he was thankful to his former partner for having infused the mind-sharpening practice of trying to remember opening chess gambits into his watch-and-wait routine.

He returned to his surveillance of the top floor suite across the street and put one hand to his ear to better hear the conversations his mic picked up.

"I'm telling you, Pops," a young voice said. To Pain's ear, "Pops" didn't sound like someone addressing his father or grandfather in a friendly, familiar way. It sounded like someone ready to kick an old man to the curb. He turned the volume up.

"It's time we got more aggressive in our dealings," the young voice continued and he mentally assigned the younger speaker the name Punk—*Pops and Punk*. He smiled. *Let's see how this plays out.*

"We have been dealing with your friends down south for so long," Punk said and Pain knew he was talking about the South

American cartels, "that we have forgotten they are not the only game in town. We need to get more aggressive with them."

"Aggressive in what way?" Pops asked. "Why the need to suddenly become aggressive with friends?"

"There are no such things as friends," the young gang member said. "Only suppliers. And I have made contact with the Africans who say they can supply us at half the cost."

"Oh," the Camorra leader replied, "I did not know you had been in contact with a Nigerian prince who wants us to help him regain the opium fields his uncle has willed to him."

From the youngster's silence, Pain had the feeling the comment had struck fairly close to the truth.

"We need to be able to continue to provide quality merchandise," the older man continued. "Otherwise, profits will dry up. We must always follow the path to the highest profits."

The path to the highest profits. He chuckled. *I'll have to remember that one.*

"The only problem with that philosophy," he said and chuckled at both the idea and the fact that they wouldn't hear him, "is that it might not be good enough to keep you alive."

Although if he were a betting man, he would put his money on Pops outliving Punk.

Out of ingrained training, Pain switched to his second scope that was trained on the entrance to the same building. Fle-Noir, one of the most popular clubs in the city, was located on the first floor and business dealings that were beyond the concerns of any of the club's patrons were held a few floors above.

"What's this now?" he muttered. When he was in the company of others, he always kept his thoughts to himself. But while on a stakeout when he had no one else to talk to, he tended to speak his thoughts. If he ever had an auditory response from another Pain in the room, he would have sought professional help. That not being the case in this instance, he put therapy off for another time and focused on the door at the entry to the club. Even though it was still early evening, it already had a line waiting to gain entrance.

His gaze settled on a woman who approached the entrance. Her cop's eyes were set in a face that some might call severe, but he preferred severe over soft and thought she was gorgeous. He hadn't kept up with the latest trend in hairstyles, but the short-shorn Annie Lenox look must be making a comeback. On her, with her almost black hair, it looked good.

The long coat could conceal several weapons. He wouldn't have bet against it as he watched her weave through to the front of the line. She was taller than most of the women and half of the men. He put her at five-eleven.

"You're obviously here on business," he muttered. "Please be smart and don't let it interfere with mine."

His ruminations on the Scotch Opening forgotten, he watched as she arrived at the rope and saw the bouncer nod, although his hand didn't open the rope until he'd made a call. He kept his eye on the door but his mic remained focused on the upstairs office, the voices not always clear. The bouncer's call must have been answered because one of the youngsters announced, "The Bitch is here."

Okay. He made a note of the players so far. *I've got Pops, the Punk, the Bouncer, and the Bitch.*

"Bring her up," Pops instructed.

That decision was met by a jumble of voices, none of them sounding happy, mixed with a few catcalls and whistles. The order was followed through and another bouncer appeared. The rope was lowered, the new man escorted the Bitch inside, and Pain returned his whole focus to the camera focused on the office.

Darkened windows did nothing to prevent his P-59 lens from having a clear view, although it did cast everything and everyone inside in a soft yellow glow. Again, the voices within were hard to make out. He would need to upgrade his mic soon. His current one was fine when only one voice spoke at a time but not so fine when several spoke at once.

His lens, however, worked to perfection, although he didn't like what he saw. There seemed to be unified movement and positioning and he was certain that each player was armed. The Bitch wasn't his responsibility but he'd never cared for the sight of lambs being led to the slaughter. Then again, maybe he was wrong. Maybe it was nothing more than setting up for intimidation purposes.

That hopeful thought disappeared when he heard one voice ask, "Who shall we use to clean the mess up?"

"Fuck." This time, he didn't mumble. While he didn't know anything about the Bitch, he knew Pops and the Punks were not good people. It therefore seemed logical that if they intended to eliminate her, she must be good people. Of course, he reminded himself after a moment's reflection, she might also be the competition and equally bad.

Still, his instincts leaned toward the former—and yes, it might have been because he wanted to believe she was good. Either way, he couldn't simply stand back and watch it unfold because his first perception might be the right one. He didn't always have a choice but when he did, he tried to come down on the side of good. *Stay righteous, my friend,* a voice from his past told him.

Pain got busy being righteous. Cursing the entire time, he scrambled to pack and stow all his gear except the mic and carried it to the roof. He knew a dumpster in the alley wasn't scheduled to be emptied for another three days, which should give him more than enough time to retrieve his gear. After a hasty look below, he tossed the locked case over the edge and didn't relish the prospect of the shit he would have to dig through to get it.

He ran to the front of the building. "Fuck the United States government and the heads-up-their-own ass's bureaucratic agencies! Piss on the Camorra. May they all die in a boiling vat of alfredo sauce!"

Hastily, he strapped himself into his harness. It had taken him three weeks to set up the zip-line to the building across the street and this was not how he had wanted to use it. The line itself was as strong as steel but made of a high-density nylon hybrid that would not conduct electricity, which allowed him to use the existing power lines as the runners.

"You'd better have deep pockets, Bitch. This shit is not cheap and if I have to waste it to save you, a little financial remuneration will be expected."

Pain stopped his cursing for long enough to listen in and reassess the situation across the street. If things went south, she might also owe him for the mic he had left working. Even though his cameras were packed and waiting for him in a dumpster, he still needed the mic to be able to listen as the situation unfolded. It made no sense to make an overly dramatic entrance when no actual drama was being acted out.

"Welcome, Ms. Goni," Pops said. "To what do we owe this pleasure?"

The Bitch's name is Joni? She didn't look like a Joni. It simply didn't occur to him that it might be a G that carried the softer pronunciation like that in giraffe rather than a J.

Agony had been in the club many times before but always as an officer of the law when she reminded them that they were never too far from her sight. She had often thought about hitting the club in her off-hours to dance the night away, but it was never a good idea to become too friendly with her enemies. In her line of work, trying to combine business with pleasure seldom ended up as a positive experience.

She scrutinized the main floor as she passed through and

followed the bouncer to one of the two open staircases that led to the second floor. The Fle-Noir presented two different personas on alternating nights while open. One night would be for dancing—flashing lights, ear-numbing music, and a floor filled with gyrating bodies dancing to the throbbing beats.

This evening, it was nothing but chill sleekness. It wasn't uncommon for two people who had hooked up on the dance floor the night before to return and have a conversation since talking was seldom possible while the music blared.

Even though this was a subdued night, she noted that the amount of muscle was about the same as it was on the dance nights. In addition to the bouncers, there were also several hard-looking men who all appeared to be on the clock. She had had her suspicions that the relationship between the Camorra and the Columbians had not been as smooth as it used to be. There might be pressure coming from the Mexicans, and you never knew what move the friends across the pond in Russia or whatever African nation might decide to make.

Agony thought that might bode well for her. She was only there to courteously present a simple request, which was to let her go about her business. Since they already had so much else to concern themselves with, why would they want to seek out trouble where there was none to be found? *One less thing for them to worry about, right?* She hoped they would see the logic in that.

The established procedure had been for the bouncers to lead the way up the stairs and have the supplicant follow, but since she was a regular visitor and knew the way, he let her take the lead up the stairs and trailed behind. Speaking of behind, even though her long coat prevented a detailed look at it, she knew the bouncer's main incentive for his "ladies first" politeness was that it gave him a chance to study her ass the whole way up the two flights.

When they reached the top floor, the bouncer took the lead

again, rapped twice lightly, opened the door, and retreated quietly.

"Come in, come in." Augusto Zaza greeted her. "Welcome, Ms. Goni. To what do we owe this pleasure?"

Her instincts kicked in and she studied the room hastily. Everyone seemed to stand to one side—and it certainly wasn't her side. Each man also appeared to hold one hand out of sight, which was never a good sign.

"Oh, come on, Gus." She used her pet name for the elder head of the Camorra, even though she had always known it annoyed him. Almost as soon as she said it, though, she berated herself mentally for teasing him when she no longer had a badge. She also didn't give herself any extra points for having walked into an unknown situation when she had no backup to call.

On the rooftop across the street, even though he couldn't see through the darkened windows, he reminded himself that only one person was talking at a time, at least. The girl had chutzpah, he had to give her that. He knew Augusto Zaza didn't like being called Gus any more than he would have appreciated him calling him Pops.

"You are no longer in possession of a badge, Ms. Goni," the man responded. "So you no longer pose the danger you once did when you caused so many of my business interests such temporary inconveniences."

Agony didn't know whether to scuffle her feet in an "awe shucks" gesture or to bow. "It was never anything personal." She decided on a slight smile. "I was merely a working girl, trying to do her job."

"We have a lot of working girls," one of the punks cut in. "You wanna sign up and you'll make a lot more money than you ever got wearing a badge."

"With your looks," another voice added, "we can start you in middle management. That way you can start on top."

"Or maybe," the first punk asked, "you prefer being on the bottom?"

"Rispetto!" Zaza silenced the chiding and the laugher.

"Even with a badge, Augusto"—she remembered that she was there to ask a favor and not to bust his balls—"I was never able to do you any serious damage."

"This is true, Ms. Goni." The old man nodded. "That is because I am Zaza. As you are well aware, my name consists of only two letters in the alphabet. The first and the last. I will be there at the beginning and I will be there at the end. You are simply one of the many minor letters jumbled up in the middle."

"Yes, Augusto, that's exactly what I am. Jumbled up in the middle."

"So, Ms. Goni in the Middle with no badge and not seeking employment, please answer my initial question. To what do we owe this pleasure?"

"I am a private detective now, Gus," she replied evenly, "working on a missing persons case. It is not related to you at all but might mean I have to come into your territory to ask some people a few questions. I simply wanted to let you know that my only interest is in finding this person and I hope you will allow me to do that."

"Who is this person?" Zaza asked. "Perhaps I may be able to assist?"

"You're offering to help?" Assistance from him was the last thing she was looking for.

He shrugged, "It can't hurt, can it?"

"Gus, with you, it can always hurt."

"Sadly, that is true." The man sighed and displayed his pistol, the signal for everyone else in the room to do the same.

Agony had expected some rude treatment from the youngsters and at worst, a resounding no from their leader. An outright execution was on an entirely different menu.

"I wish it were not so." He seemed to think she at least

deserved an explanation. "Someone has put out a contract on your charming head, specifying dead. The contract includes money, of course, and a certain amount of leeway while pursuing my various business interests. In other words, Ms. Goni, it pains me to inform you that whoever is after you is from your side of the tracks, not mine. That is the most painful form of betrayal."

"And it's also very annoying," she admitted, "but I'm not surprised. You don't have to do this, Gus."

"As you stated earlier, this is simply business. Nothing personal. We have been friends, yes?"

"Friends?" Agony could raise her guns but she could also do one hell of a job with an eyebrow.

"Call us amicable enemies, then." Zaza shrugged. "But more freedom of movement along with the money? We took the offer."

"That's a shame." She was being honest. "Out of all of them, I had truly hoped you'd be the one to live long enough to enjoy the gangster fantasy of being able to retire to a small villa with good wine, a fat wife, and a skinny mistress."

"From your mouth to God's ears." He stopped short of adding an amen. "It has been an occasional pleasure knowing you, Ms. Goni. You are as hard as they come but no one is bulletproof."

She knew she would only have the time to draw and fire one shot before her body was riddled. Sentiment toward Gus led her to focus on the smarmiest of the youngsters who had taunted her earlier.

Agony paused for a second before she drew her weapon. Nope, it wasn't her imagination. Everyone present showed that they had heard the commotion coming from the hallway on the other side of the door. It was the sound of what might be a two-hundred-pound object bouncing off the walls and the door.

"What the hell is this?" Zaza squinted as he looked at her. "You are no longer a cop so you have no backup."

While she was fully and painfully aware of that, she shrugged and hoped the cold smile that now played across her lips distracted everyone from her shifting her weight to the proper footing and tensing her muscles in hopeful preparation for impending violence.

"Stuvo. Nahman," the Camorra leader ordered. "Tend to the door."

Stuvo was the first to reach it and as he placed his hand on the knob, about to turn it, his arm was broken when the door burst open. It also did no favors to the young punk's face.

From her angle, Agony couldn't see the kick to the crotch but Nahman screamed, doubled over, and fell. There could be no doubt about his distress but many doubts as to whether he would ever be able to produce enough functional sperm to continue his family line.

Everyone froze for a moment, not quite sure what to make of the intruder, but he certainly fell on the foe side of the friend or foe equation.

A short second later, all hell broke loose, but Agony and her cop's eyes absorbed a slew of details.

The intruder was several inches taller than her and powerfully built. With no visible strain or effort, he held one of the hard men she had seen downstairs across his chest and heaved the bruiser into the group of mobsters who stood in a line against the wall with their guns drawn.

How did you judge a face in a split second? If there was an island in the middle of the Mediterranean Sea, the face could have embodied it—from Spain to Italy, from the Middle East to Egypt, and skipping along the North African coast to Morocco. Only one thing was certain. He would never be mistaken for a Scandinavian.

It also revealed enough scuff and gauntness to testify that he had been living ragged for a while, a look that seemed to suit him. His dark eyes held nothing but danger and a gleam that said he was more than willing to get a little wild should the occasion call for it.

The body that had been tossed into those along the wall made three of the men tumble. Agony used the moment of communal shock to kick a gaudy fake fountain off an end table and into the face of the youngster still standing who had the cleanest line of sight to her. She drew one of the sidearms her long coat had concealed and fired the first shot.

At that point, the fun began in earnest.

CHAPTER TWO

Pain had enough firearms training to be able to bring down a chopper blindfolded and with behind-the-back shots using only a Glock but the truth was that he didn't like them. He didn't like to fire them and disliked it even more when they were fired at him. There was something impersonal about being able to cause death from a distance. When it came to disablement, dismemberment, or death, he was much more of a touchy-feely kind of guy.

Even though he preferred violence to be up close and personal, that didn't mean he wasn't aware that many people he would come up against didn't share his distaste for firearms. The under-armor suit he wore next to his skin was a testimony to modern technology. Kevlar vests were wonderful and functional for those who had access to them, but comparing them to his protective suit was like comparing payphones to the latest version of whatever cell phone had been released on the market.

It was comprised of hard and soft layers and he wasn't completely convinced that the government he used to work for hadn't stolen the technology from aliens still held in Area Fifty-one. Bullets and knives couldn't pierce it. They could cause painful bruises but the suit itself would remain undamaged.

Unfortunately, it didn't give him any kind of super-human strength. If someone was able to get close enough, they could try to dislocate a shoulder, break an arm, or disable one of his knees with a kick to the relevant joint. But someone delivering death from a distance would need a headshot and when fighting, his head was never in the same place for longer than the flap of a hummingbird's wing so it would have to be one hell of a shot.

Agony, on the other hand, had no aversion to being on the right side of a gun but had only fired hers twice to kill in the line of duty while wearing a badge. In both instances, it had come down to either her or them. Not that she hadn't fired a few times to disable and very successfully too, but she only had two kill-shots to her name.

While still on the force, she had started working out in an MMA gym she still managed to visit to train at least twice a week. She also never left home without her collapsible baton. Disarm and disable before dealing out death was one of her mantras. Lately, she'd found it harder to find sparring partners in the gym. She was extremely agile and lightning-fast, able to deliver a kick to the head while upside down and at the same time, land a fist blow on the little toe.

The boots they wore while in the octagon were soft and flexible and no one ever expected a solid blow to the little toe. She had invented the move herself. Body shots and headshots were so routine that they could be shrugged off. But if someone walked through their house and caught their little toe on the edge of a table or a chair, the whole body shook with pain. She had learned to attack the most vulnerable and unexpected parts of her opponent's body.

Zaza, for all his authority, was not used to holding a gun in his hand. He had hired help for that. When the chaos ensued, he knew that if he fired his pistol, he was more than likely to hit one of the dozen who were defending him than either of the two who were currently wreaking havoc. He decided to stay low and try to slide inconspicuously along the walls until he could reach the door and make a safe escape.

After the initial shock, the youngsters finally found enough balls to fight back. Dozens of shots rang out from the four corners of the room. The problem with that strategy was that the only ones hit by the shots were the other punks who were also firing into the center of the room where the opponents had been a second before.

When the barrage was unleashed, Pain simply dove to the floor and disjointed someone's elbow, while Agony did a handspring off a coffee table and directed a throat kick to the windpipe of someone who might or might not survive the assault but would never be able to talk in anything louder than a whisper again.

He made his first mistake after the elbow dislocation when he saw Zaza sneaking along a wall, trying to make a quiet escape. Without thought, he picked the punk up by his wrists—and caused even louder screaming due to the dislocated elbows—and swung him in a full circle before he hurled him at the Camorra leader, hoping to delay the man's escape.

In the flurry of activity, he hadn't realized that the wall Zaza was sneaking along was the window wall. Ordinarily, the body toss would have been effective and wouldn't have led to anyone's death. Even though the Camorra leader had paid for tinted windows, he hadn't sprung enough for them to be either bullet or shatterproof. They were simply tinted glass windows and he and the flung body crashed through them and followed gravity to the street below.

"What the hell?" Agony shouted at her self-appointed rescuer as shattered glass continued to fall in what seemed like slow motion behind Gus, who had been her easy-pass to discovering who had taken the hit out on her.

She shot at a punk to her right but looked to her left and screamed at the Neanderthal, "I needed him, asshole!"

"Then go get him," Pain retorted as he ducked under a fist thrown in haste and retaliated with two short staggered jabs, followed by an end of the argument right hook, "if you care so much. He shouldn't be too hard to find."

"I don't care two shits about him!" She dove behind a couch and came up firing a shot that left her with one less opponent to deal with. "But he has information I needed."

"Welcome to the club. I'll take the blame for the punk-toss but not for the cheap-ass windows."

Their spirited getting to know you conversation was interrupted when several of their adversaries—who still stood along opposite sides of the room—fired another volley aimed at the big man who stood in the middle.

Two more youngsters went down from friendly fire but so did Pain as several rounds struck him in his chest and back.

"We got him, we got him, we got him!" one cried and a cheer went up that lasted only as long as it took for him to push to his feet.

"Flesh wounds," he announced as he looked around. "Do any other punks feel lucky?"

"Fuck this shit!" a voice shouted.

All the youngsters still standing—who had imagined themselves as real badasses but had never been in a firefight before—left their wounded comrades to fend for themselves and fought with each other over who would be the first to reach the door and get the hell out of there.

Pain watched the rats scurry out and abandon ship. "It's hard to get good help these days," he said to no one in particular.

Agony picked herself up off the floor, not sure why the intruder was still alive after taking half a dozen body shots. But since he was, she intended to speak her mind.

"I don't know who the fuck you are or why you're even here."

"It seemed like there was a damsel in distress," he answered as he counted the bullet holes in his outer clothing.

"Don't ever call me a damsel!" Her mood hadn't changed much since she had watched her main source of information tumble out the window. "And don't you dare to presume to think I am ever in distress. I was doing fine until you arrived."

"Yes." He tried to work out why she was so pissed at him. "I noticed how you had them all so outnumbered."

"You threw Gus out the window."

"I did no such thing." Man, she was on the edge of becoming annoying. "All I did was throw a punk at him. The tumble out the window choreography was something they did all on their own."

"But I needed to talk to him."

"Then maybe you should have invited him to a tea party. Maybe one everyone doesn't show up to fully armed."

He had carried on the conversation as he walked around the room and examined the bodies on the floor. Some were in extreme pain, and no one could do anything for others except notify their next of kin. Out of habit, he kicked all the firearms casually out of harm's way as he moved from one to the other.

While he strolled around the room, Agony searched frantically through the drawers of Gus's desk. There must be something in there to identify which of her former law-enforcement colleagues now had it in for her. Sure, she could be a pain in the ass sometimes but nothing that was bad enough to have a hit assigned to her.

"Maybe I thought this was a tea party, jerk-off." She was tossing papers out left and right.

"Yeah, I'm sure you did, what with you being dressed in your most delicate finest."

Below in the club, the bouncers and the other security personnel isolated the Camorra youngsters who had scurried down the stairs in a side room. There was no sense in starting a panic amongst the paying customers. They also wanted to know more about the big dude who had rushed through earlier. He had left enough damage in his wake that no one was anxious to race after him without knowing more about what they would be getting into.

They had also thought that with the number of guns Zaza had defending him, dealing with one guy, no matter how big he was, shouldn't be too much of a problem.

"No, no, no!" one of the more coherent youngsters said. "You don't understand. It was like when you watch the weather channel and see a tornado ripping through some bum-fuck town somewhere. It throws houses and cars and shit in the air like popcorn and there's nothing anyone can do to stop it."

"Oh, yeah." One of the bouncers smiled. "I love watching that shit."

"Well, you wouldn't like watching it so much if you were stuck in the same fucking room with it."

At this point, the kid, whose name was Jimmy, was merely glad that he might live long enough to celebrate his twenty-second birthday.

"You had him out-gunned," Torch, the leader of the security team stated. "Why didn't you simply shoot the fucker?"

"You think we didn't try?" Jimmy's eyes were frantic. "The fucker took a dozen direct hits, fell on the floor, and got up again, looking like he was pissed that we'd ruined his shirt."

"He dove to the floor, kid," Torch responded, "because you were shooting at him. If he looked pissed it was probably only disapproval at how bad your aim was."

The other men laughed.

"You punks think you're all badasses," the leader continued, "because you're part of the Camorra Family, but that don't mean shit when bullets fly. Why don't you kiddies sit the rest of this one out and leave it to the professionals? Oh, where's Zaza?"

"He's out on the sidewalk."

"Okay, then he's safe."

"I didn't say that."

"You haven't said much of anything yet except a shit full of nothing." Torch turned to the others. "Up the stairs, two by two. No introductions—take the fucker down!"

Their survey of the room and mayhem was interrupted when some of the security men Agony had noticed during her walk through the first floor rushed through the door. Torch's crew took their jobs very seriously and all of them had been less than pleased when some big fucker had swept through the club and picked one of them up to use as a battering ram to get through the others as he rushed up the stairs.

Their intention was to shoot first and leave questions for another day. A bullet barrage followed.

Pain upended a dresser and they dove behind it. "Aim to kill," he advised.

"And what will you aim for?" she asked. "Wounds to their egos?"

"I don't do firearms."

"What the fuck?"

"Keep them distracted." He made sure his wrist band was still functional. "I'm working on our exit strategy."

He rolled away, leapt up, and snatched a glass ashtray off of the Camorra leader's desk. *Zaza always did like his cigars,* she remembered. He launched it at their opponents like a Frisbee on amphetamines and it sliced the main arteries in two necks before it came to rest in a bloody mess.

The others were left covered in arterial blood and tried to wipe it out of their eyes so they could focus on who to shoot. Her uninvited rescuer took a large framed photo of Gus's family off a wall and shattered it over the heads of two bruisers who stood too close together.

Oh, sure, she thought caustically, *that's gonna hurt.*

To her disbelief, the big guy spun what was left of the photo and the frame in a quick circle and she gasped as the glass left in the frame sliced through two more neck arteries and spewed even more blood into everyone's eyes.

There wouldn't be any more gunfire for a few seconds, so Agony surveyed the floor and saw a cell phone lying a little beyond the grasp of one of the youngsters, who might or might not still be alive. His health was not her concern but the phone was. She scrambled to retrieve it and used the thumbprint of the maybe-alive-maybe-dead youngster to access it. There wasn't enough time to scroll through all its contents so she simply started the process of sending everything to herself.

Pain punched the release code into his wristband. The people on the street, who were looking at the two bodies now sprawled on the sidewalk but were reluctant to get too close to them, heard several loud pops from the roof across the street. Their first thought was a sniper and they decided to dive to the sidewalk themselves and so missed the sight of a zip-line that swung down and now hung vertically from the roof of the club's building.

With the security detail having cleared the blood from their eyes and about to start firing again, he decided that now was not the time for explanations. He scooped Agony off the floor and she lost her hold on the cell phone—and added another item to her list of the number of things the intruder had done to piss her off. Next on the list would be the way he tossed her over his shoulder and carried her across the room before he leapt through the shattered window.

She only had a couple of seconds to scream profanities at him as she looked down and saw Gus sprawled on the sidewalk below and surrounded by a small crowd that had gathered. To her surprise, rather than hurtling to join them, they swung out into space. She had no idea where the line he hung onto with his free hand came from, but he released enough of it that when momentum swung them back toward the building, they crashed through a large window directly below Gus' office.

CHAPTER THREE

Shawn thought that one of Fle-Noir's Chill Nights would be a great time for the double-date he and Britney had set up to introduce their two friends. He had brought Melvin, a fellow junior attorney he shared an office with at Flaggett & Floggett, one of the most successful personal injury law firms in town.

Britney had dragged Katrine along, an art major from Europe who was spending two semesters at a local university. When anyone asked her as a visitor to the United States what her favorite state was, would always reply, "Catatonic, and its capital city, Catatonia, which is where I wish I was now." That often left people debating amongst themselves if that was one of the states near the Rockies or more down south.

They were seated on the second level at a window table, a location that allowed them to observe the action on the first floor or to gaze out the window should there be no excitement going on downstairs. There had been a slight commotion a few minutes earlier as some mean-looking men rushed to the floor above.

The two couples heard popping sounds along with shouts coming from the next level. Katrine had spent most of her time with Melvin trying to stifle yawns but she couldn't quash the latest one when she listened to the fun those on the floor above them seemed to be enjoying.

"Now that, up above"—she gazed at the ceiling—"sounds like a party I am sad to miss."

As it turned out, she didn't have to devise a way to crash the party since two of the party-goers crashed through the window and brought at least part of the party to her.

A large man landed on his back in the middle of the table and scattered plates and drinks as a long, lean woman landed face-down on top of him. The woman looked at the two couples as she brandished a handgun and with a snarl, advised them, "You might not want to wait for dessert."

"Oh, my God!" Britney shouted, "It's *The Rock!*" She spun toward Shawn. "You didn't tell me that we would be in a movie. I would have done something different with my hair!"

Agony looked at the man she was straddling.

"I've been told there is a resemblance." Pain shrugged.

That was one hell of a stunt, my man," Melvin shouted. "So it's true that you don't use stunt-doubles?"

"What the fuck have you kids been drinking?" Agony shouted at them.

"Are you a stunt double or the lead actress?" Melvin searched for a cocktail napkin and a pen to get some autographs.

"What I am," she informed them, "is a woman who is about to put an end to your pitiful young life."

She flipped her gun and used the butt of the pistol to rearrange the idiot's nose.

The two couples finally got the message and ran screeching down the closest staircase, Melvin's shriek much higher and louder than the others. The end result was that a general panic was triggered on the main floor when a reality that one didn't normally find in a nightclub settled in. The stampede for the main entrance built up so quickly that the bouncers barely had time to get out of its way before they were trampled underfoot.

Pain, still flat on his back on the table, looked at the attractive woman who lay face-down on top of him and held the barrel of her sidearm an inch above his face. It was an American brand, not European.

"Don't you ever do that again." She growled belligerently.

She could feel the rumble in his chest when he chuckled. "Do what? Save your life twice? Okay, I get your point. The first time should have been enough to impress you. The second time was probably overkill. I can be kind of an asshole sometimes."

An unexpected ring tone—"The Macarena," of all things— from somewhere inside the woman's coat prevented her response. She scowled, opened a flap of the coat enough to slide her hand in, checked a small screen, and shut the ring tone off.

Her device had informed her that even though she no longer had access to the youngster's phone, all its content had been uploaded to a private cloud service that she paid a hefty price for to store the files from her cases.

"That's a shame." She sighed as she raised her gun. "I had almost hoped for an excuse to use this on you."

"I understand." Pain recognized her frustration. "I often have that effect on women."

With a black look, she climbed off him and they both found solid footing on the floor. She went to what was left of the window and looked at the sidewalk to see what was left of Gus' body. To her amazement, Zaza was mobile. The punk must have hit the pavement first and broken the old man's fall.

Although certainly a little battered and wobbly, he tried to sneak quietly out of a startled crowd who also seemed to be trying to gain their feet.

"Son of a bitch, Zaza," she said in wonder. "You must be half-cat to have so many lives."

Sirens and flashing blue lights racing toward the scene caught her and everyone else's attention.

"Sonofabitch!"

Pain heard the sirens and needed only one guess as to the color of the lights.

"What? Those aren't friends of yours?" Having paid attention to all the earlier conversations, he already knew the answer to that question. She used to carry a shield and if he had to make a guess, it would be that she carried it damn well—probably too well for her own good.

She stepped away from the window, knowing she had no friends among those who approached. A handful of security men and pride-wounded punks looked at her from the first floor, not to mention that the office above still held many of the hard men still alive above her. She was fresh out of friends.

Speculatively, she studied the intruder with her cop's eyes, noted his equipment and his nonchalant stance, and remembered how he had handled himself in a complex situation he had not been invited to.

"I have had dealings with all the Alphabet Agencies." It sounded abrupt because she had no time to waste. "And you are not a part of any of them."

Pain merely nodded so she continued. "That means that you are either part of a private group or a freelancer and so far, seem to be in no hurry to see my ass toasted."

"You're two for two so far," he assured her.

"So please tell me you have a place to go to ground."

"Define ground."

They both heard the commotion on the stairs. The security team had no doubt finally removed the blood from their eyes and rushed down from what was left of Zaza's office. When they glanced at the floor below them, the stampede had thinned and the Camorra leader's third line of security forces now emerged from wherever they'd been secluded. They seemed to prefer semi-automatic RK's over handguns.

Agony didn't want to debate the definition of ground at that moment.

"Do you at least have a vehicle nearby?"

"Define vehicle."

"Wheels!" she shouted.

"Define nearby."

Damn, the man was infuriating. He possessed all the calmness of someone who was about to tell her that all they had to do was step out of the window they had crashed through and that he had a private helicopter waiting to whisk them up and away from the fray.

"Nearby as in closer than the back alley of this shithole?" She glowered at him and thought she might have seen the first glint of panic in his eyes.

"If you have one parked that close, we won't need mine." He shrugged.

"Well, I'm glad that's settled." She raised her gun level with his head and fired two quick shots. Each one whistled past his ears, one on the left and one on the right.

He spun and his startled gaze settled on two armed men who had tried to sneak behind him. As he pulled a grenade out, he swiveled his head slightly to smile at her.

"Are you shitting me? You said you didn't carry guns."

"Does this look like a gun to you? When was the last time you had a piggyback ride?"

Pain turned so his back was to her.

And I thought this day couldn't get any stranger. Agony gritted her teeth, clambered on, and held her breath as the man tossed the grenade. She then held on for dear life as he leapt out the window. He caught the line they had swung in on and pulled them both, hand over hand, into Zaza's office.

Once there, he asked calmly, "Now, which way to your car?"

She frowned at him and waited for the grenade to explode.

"It was merely a little noxious smoke grenade. They won't be able to see through it and it might be a couple of days before their eyes stop watering. Now, it's your turn. Please tell me there is a back exit."

Another burst of gunfire from below ceased quickly when everyone on the lower floors realized they were all firing blindly. Most of them attempted to shield their eyes.

Agony led him to the fire escape that took them to the alley ten feet from where she'd left her ride.

"I didn't peg you as a soccer mom," Pain observed as he climbed into the minivan.

"Well then, I guess you were wrong for once." She drove to the end of the alley and tried to decide which way to turn to provide her with the fastest route out of Dodge. She'd almost made her mind up when her passenger insisted that they had to circle to the building across the street.

"Are you out of your fucking mind? The whole street is a clusterfuck and we have to get far away as fast as possible."

"I need to retrieve my gear." He didn't sound like he was giving her an option.

"What gear?"

"The gear I abandoned when I so rudely rescued you."

"Oh, so now you're pulling a guilt trip?"

"Spoken like a true soccer mom to a child strapped into a back seat. Please." For the first time, she heard a plea in his voice. "I have to retrieve my gear. I am on a Quest and can't complete it without my equipment."

Now was not the time nor did Pain know her well enough to explain The Quest, but he had to retrieve his case from the dumpster. It held more than fancy surveillance gear. Some of the equipment held information he had gathered and he needed it in the most desperate of ways.

Against every instinct in her body, she turned left and stopped in front of a fire hydrant a short distance from the corner. He gave her no further explanations and simply jumped out, ran half a block ahead, and disappeared down the alley behind the building across from Zaza's.

From her vantage point, she could see that the block to the left in front of Fle-Noir was already packed with police cars and ambulances. All traffic from the side street was being directed to either go straight or turn right. She wanted to turn right and speed away from the chaos but she'd had a partner before. Even though she wanted to be rid of this one as soon as they were both safe, she felt an ingrained cop obligation to wait.

She waited, parked illegally in front of a hydrant while all hell broke loose on the main street, and argued with herself.

Hit the pedal girl, turn right, and get the fuck out of here.

You never leave a partner behind.

I don't remember you informing the big fuck that you needed a partner.

But if I was taking applications for a partner, he has some dangerous abilities that could put him in the running.

So does King Kong, but do you honestly think you could afford the food to feed him? Not to mention having to clean his shit up if you took him for a walk through the city park. He doesn't even carry a gun. Is that the kind of partner you want to cover your back?

King Kong never needed a gun.

A sharp rap on her window and a bright light in her eyes suddenly silenced the other thirty-four people who seemed to be crowded into the back of her minivan.

Agony shook her head swiftly, summoned her sweetest, most innocent smile, rolled her window down, and tried to shield her eyes from the flashlight that shined in them. She managed to block out enough of the glare to be able to see the officer's badge. *R. Ogg.*

"Ma'am," Officer Ogg informed her in a voice that held neither suspicion nor animosity, "you need to move your vehicle out of this space."

"Sorry, Officer." She had never been very good at a confused and innocent voice but she gave it her best attempt. "Am I doing something wrong?"

"Well, ma'am." At a guess, he had probably been on the force for only six months and tried to sound gentle but firm. "You are currently parked in front of a fire hydrant and we might need access to it, given that we are currently dealing with a situation."

His partner approached slowly from behind him and turned to wave a looky-loo woman on. The officer's scowl suggested that he hated the looky-loos. The girl probably had one hand on the wheel and one hand holding a cell phone and was no doubt filming all the commotion on the street in front of Fle-Noir to post later on her social media page.

Ogg's partner's wave became a little more firm when the driver of the older, beige sedan didn't move on as quickly as she should have. Her father had probably made the down payment on the trash heap of a car so his daughter wouldn't have to rely on public transportation and there she was, all la-di-da-ing while the police had a job to do.

"I'm sorry, Officer." Agony looked as flustered as possible. "One of my girlfriends came to the Noir to have a drink with someone she met online. It was her first night out in the real world after catching her husband in their bed with one of his co-workers and she kicked his ass out and swore to never trust another man again."

"That does sound like an all too familiar story," Officer Ogg agreed. "Nonetheless, I need you to move along now."

"I would love to, Officer." She pleaded unashamedly now. "She texted me that her date was going great and I sent her a thumbs-up. A little later, she called me and said that all hell was breaking loose and she needed a ride home and didn't want to trust a guy she had met online. I rushed down here and only need to wait until she can find me."

"Ma'am..." The young man glanced at the minivan. He had heard so many similarly painful housewives' stories that he had all the sympathy in the world for the driver's friend, but he still had a job to do and the situation was escalating. "Ma'am," he repeated, "I need you to please move along. Your friend will have to find her own way home."

Where the fuck is he? Agony could only stall for so long. The second man waved a few more cars through and stepped up behind him. His entire demeanor said he was tired of doing ride-along's with rookies and that with six months under his belt, Ogg should have learned how to move a whiney suburban woman along by now.

She tried to smile at the newcomer and maintain her some-what desperate friend persona but he shined his flashlight in her eyes and she had to shield them. The beam revealed her face only as long as was necessary before he swept it over the rest of her. It lingered on her coat when the light picked up some sparkles from tiny pieces of glass and what might have been a spot of blood or two.

He tapped Officer Ogg's ankle quickly with his boot and a second later, she faced two Department Issued S & W's not aimed with the intent to disarm or disable. They were aimed with the intent to drop with all severity if she made one wrong move.

The right move, of course, was to trust her partner, asshole though he might be and at least give him a chance to prove that he had her back. She lifted her hands off the wheel.

"Hands off the wheel! Hands off the wheel!" Officer Ogg shouted.

Agony, her hands still raised, addressed the officer she had not yet been introduced to. "I can see there is a rookie here and my guess is it isn't you."

"Your guess is correct, ma'am," the young man's training partner informed her. "My name is Randolf, five years on the force. Will you please step out of the vehicle now?"

He even took the precaution to open the door so he could keep both her hands in sight.

She had a decision to make. The first was to accelerate, get the hell out of there, and hope she could reach the train station. From there, she could catch a train to a town on the other side of nowhere and rebuild her life as a waitress in a Waffle House who called all her customers, Hon or Sug. The second was that she could surrender and be taken into custody, while those in the force who had taken a contract out on her found a way to eventually have her executed during an escape attempt or some other fabricated altercation.

How did it come to this? All she had wanted from this day was to talk to Gus and let him know she was working as a PI on a missing persons case and assure him that she wouldn't step on any of his toes while she pursued it.

Now, all she wanted to do was let go with a sigh and wonder which fork in the road of her life had she chosen to follow the wrong tine on?

CHAPTER FOUR

"The pedal on the left means stop. The pedal on the right means go. At this moment, I would advise using the pedal on the right," Pain stated calmly.

"What the fuck?" Agony agreed with the advice but she was still trying to wrap her head around the cheerfully efficient way her partner-who-wasn't had disabled both officers without them even realizing he was there.

He tossed something weighty into the back of the minivan before he slid into the shotgun seat and strapped his seat belt on. She looked in her side-view mirror to where the rookie and his training ride-along rolled on the street, clutched their legs, and moaned in pain.

"I suggest a sharp right turn, Joni, followed by a steadily increasing pressure on the right pedal but not enough to draw any undue attention."

She took the first part of that advice and turned right as the scent of rotting fruit filled her olfactory senses.

"Fucking organic coops." He apologized for the smell that had followed him into the soccer-mom-mobile. "They always wait until the last minute before they throw their spoiled fruit into the dumpster. It was like a fucking compost pile in there."

Pain hadn't had time to rinse his equipment off after he retrieved it.

"At every moment," he continued ruefully while she focused on making steady progress away from the recent fray, "I expected plantains to sprout out my left ear while bananas jumped out my right. Now that would be a battle worth beholding—trees full of plantains on the left and bananas on the right, battling to see who deserved to be eaten first. "

The smell, she realized, didn't come from the big man but from the case he had dumped in the back of her soccer-mom-mobile. For a brief moment, she wondered if her passenger had access to the legendary Electrical Bananas. That would certainly explain his lapses in the mental cognitive ability to panic when he had to focus on the danger he seemed to be in at any given moment since she'd met him.

Agony looked in her rearview mirror and realized that they had managed to escape the perimeter her former comrades in blue had established.

"Is there any particular direction we should head in?" she asked calmly and kept her foot light on the pedal on the right.

"Any direction that begins with north, Joni," the big man replied. "I need to get my bearings."

"Your bearings?" She fought the urge to thrust the pedal on the right through the fucking floor until they ran out of road, next stop Canada. "What do you mean you need to get your bearings? And why the fuck do you keep calling me Joni?"

"Until a short time ago," he answered blithely, "all my bearings were focused on the two buildings that are no longer accessible. They were the center. But if you keep heading north, I'm fairly sure I can remember how to get to an old safe place of mine."

"Fairly sure?" She was not particularly reassured by that statement. "I thought you were a damn professional and fairly sure falls far from a professional's response. Do you know where we're going or not?"

"I do." The big man's head maintained a slow swivel from side to side, but his gaze seemed to be in constant motion. "But it's been a while since the last time I was in town. When I returned to pursue The Quest, I set up shop in a small room across the street from your pal Zaza."

Even though she thought they'd escaped the immediate danger zone and she made sure to stay under the posted speed limit, Agony couldn't help but flinch and wince every time she passed a parked set of flashing blue lights. She had no idea if Ogg or his partner had put out a BOLO for a dark minivan but so far, none of the blue lights had pulled out to follow her. She congratulated herself on her choice of rides yet again. Minivans were still one of the most ubiquitous vehicles on any given street.

"So, you set up shop across from Zaza," she echoed to refocus on her questions while she did her best to maintain a course that was mostly north. "And let's get this clear—Zaza is not my pal."

"Yeah," he replied, his gaze never still. "I was able to work that out from the number of guns he had waiting to greet you."

"And what the fuck does the old bastard have to do with your Quest? Did the two of you play online versions of Dungeons and Dragons together during your misspent youth?"

"The years of my youth were never misspent, Joni," he replied casually. "The years of my adulthood, on the other hand…"

The tone of his voice might have sounded casual, but she could sense a razor-thin edge of alertness and paranoia in his movements. It was as if he expected some kind of danger to appear at any second, even though they had now left the blue lights far behind.

"Before this goes any further…" She had to get at least one of her questions answered. "Why the fuck do you keep calling me Joni?"

He reached into the back seat, snapped open his case that

smelled like rotten fruit, and began to rummage through it. "Because that's what Pops called you."

"Who the hell is Pops?"

"I call him Pops. Pops and the Punks. You call him Gus. Maybe Gus and the Goons? A Zaza by any other name would still smell as bad, although it would make a great line-up for a Battle of the Bands Night at a local club. On stage number one…" He switched to his best imitation of an MC's voice. "We have Pops and the Punks. On stage number two, Gus and the Goons. Vomit on the floor to cast your votes for your favorite."

He seemed to have found what he was looking for and although he didn't pull it out and display it on his lap, he placed it directly behind his seat for easy access.

"Look…" She tried to keep her eyes on the road instead of on his movements. "I don't know why you think he called me Joni—" She gave herself a mental kick in the ass for not having realized it sooner. "Shit! You listened in on the whole conversation."

She realized that Gus' pronunciation of Goni would have come out sounding like Joni.

"What conversation?" Pain made a valiant attempt to sound thoroughly confused, even though he sensed that they both used this as fall-back positions when they knew the ploy for what it was.

"Let's start over with the names, shall we? Nothing formal." She extended her hand. "I'm not sure I want to trust you with my actual name yet, but my former co-workers simply call me Agony."

Pain had been a co-worker of hers for less than an hour but he could easily understand how she could have earned that moniker. He took her hand. "My name is Pain." He recalled the earlier ring tone from inside her coat. "Macarena Pain."

"Macarena? Who names a child Macarena?"

"You'd have to know my parents." He smiled. "Call me Pain for now."

"I'm almost pleased to meet you, Mister Pain For Now."

Agony was the first to release the greeting handshake when she returned the hand to the wheel.

She finally reached an entrance ramp to a four-lane divided highway that ran north-south and took the northbound ramp onto a road that she hoped wouldn't end in a cul-de-sac of flashing blue lights.

"We are now officially heading due north," she informed him as she accelerated and merged into traffic, pleased to finally be able to apply a little more pressure to the pedal on the right. "How far north do we have to go before your memory is jogged enough to direct us to your—our—safe place?"

"That depends." She noted that suddenly, there was no note of nonchalance in his voice.

"Depends on what?" The tension in him was contagious.

"On how long it takes you to lose the slightly used beige sedan that's tailed us ever since I tossed my gear in and we made our oh-so-discreet exit from the chaos at the Noir."

Agony glanced in her mirror and scowled when she located a beige sedan two cars behind. She might have chalked it up to his slightly elevated paranoid state if she hadn't remembered a similar car being waved along by Officer Ogg's partner. The vehicle had rolled past her a little slower than it should have and she remembered the young woman driver's face—a face that should have been more focused on the street in front of her than on her.

"Best guess..." He pulled the equipment he'd recently stashed behind his seat onto his lap. "Do you think they're here for you or me?"

"Your guess is as good as mine." She started a series of maneuvers to help her confirm what their level of paranoia should be. "I saw a similar car when I waited for you on the corner. If it's the same one, it only had a young woman driving and no backseat passengers unless they had been ducking down and hiding."

Agony cut into the left lane and increased speed. A few minutes later, she changed lanes again and eased into the right lane flow. After a moment, she veered into the left lane again and accelerated to pass a few cars before she swung into the slow lane and rode the bumper of a semi.

The driver of the beige car was cautious and followed all trailing protocols, but Pain had been right. They were being followed.

"She lost her buffer space," she informed him although she assumed he already knew that. "She is now the first car behind us."

"Nice driving there." He tossed her a compliment that sounded sincere. "Now carry on as if you don't know that she's tailing us, but try to not lose her."

"Try to not lose her?" What the hell was he talking about? "Don't put this shit all on me, Pain for Now! It's her job to not lose us, not mine to not lose her."

Pain finally finished fumbling in his bag and pulled out what looked like the bastard son of a shotgun mic and a video camera, although she wouldn't bet against the ray-gun aspect of the contraption having come from the red-headed-son of the mailman.

"Who wants you dead?" he asked. "And I mean dead, like now, other than Zaza and the entire eastern seaboard Camorra connections?"

"Do you ask all the girls this or am I merely that special?" she quipped in a sickly-sweet voice. "And what exactly do you plan to do with that, Captain Kirk? Is it the latest technology to use while beaming someone up?"

"Age of the car?" He fiddled with a lever. "The over-under is ten years."

She looked in the rearview mirror. "It's too close to call."

"I thought you were a professional." He was distracted by his levers but not enough to deliver a slightly mocking echo of her earlier statement to him.

"A professional what?" she demanded, all glibness gone as she glanced angrily at him. "A professional used car salesman?"

"Over-under!" Pain had no glibness left either. "Ten years?"

Agony looked in the mirror. "Under. Definitely under." She had made her bet. Now, she would have to lie in it.

He rolled his window down and hauled half his upper body along with his contraption out into the air.

"What the fuck are you doing?" Agony shouted. "Preparing to abandon ship when things are getting fun?"

"Hold her steady!" he shouted in response.

Or... She entertained the thought briefly. *I could jerk into the left lane so you tumble out of the window and leave you to fend for yourself.*

Agony chose to hold her steady and didn't hear a shot. All she heard were horns blaring while in her rearview mirror, she watched the beige sedan suddenly decelerate and pull off the side of the road. All vehicles behind it had to swerve to avoid a collision as it came to rest under an overpass.

She also pulled to the side of the road as Pain contorted himself through the window and into the shotgun seat again. Without a word, he reconfigured his weapon, stowed it in its bag, and replaced it carefully in the rotten-produce-smelling container.

"Nice shot," she congratulated him.

"Practice, practice, practice," was all his modesty would allow him to say before he felt the minivan slow. "This is the part of the story," he informed her, "where Kirk says, 'Floor it, Scotty, and get us the hell out of here!'"

"Oh, crap," She came to a stop on the shoulder of the highway "I must have missed that episode."

She put her vehicle in reverse and backed up slowly along the shoulder toward the now-disabled sedan.

"What part of full speed ahead," he asked with exaggerated patience, "isn't clear?"

"The part," she replied calmly as she continued slowly in reverse, "that is missing the never leave a stranded motorist in distress."

Agony put the minivan in park but left the engine running in case she was about to make a terrible judgment call. It wouldn't be her first and she didn't want to leave a partner, however new, stranded by keeping the keys in her pocket.

"I merely need to see if we can offer her any assistance." She turned and met Macarena Pain's gaze. "And while I do that, try to search your fried banana brain and remember where the fuck your safe place is. But first, I need you to give me your word, with whatever oath you hold most sacred, that you will not drive off without me."

"My word is my oath. I'm somewhat old-fashioned that way. And I give you my word that I will not leave you stranded."

She saw no lie in his eyes and gave him a smile that let him know that she had every confidence in the world that he had never fried a brain cell in his life except, maybe, while playing too many Quest games. But they could put that discussion on hold for another day.

"Here!" He stopped her and held out what looked like a small flashlight. "Keep your pistol in your left hand—your non-dominant hand—and keep this in your right."

"What is this?" She frowned at it.

"It's kind of a stun gun," Pain explained quickly. "It only has one button and its only purpose is to fire. Keep your gun in plain view so whoever is in the sedan will focus on that. If anyone is hiding in the back seat, one push of the button won't kill them but it will ruin the rest of their day. It holds six shots. Use them wisely."

She held the flashlight in her right hand and familiarized

herself with where the button was. Then, as awkward as it felt, she held her pistol in plain view in her left hand as she marched forward to have a chat to the now-stranded motorist.

CHAPTER FIVE

Agony was halfway to the sedan when she realized that he hadn't said he wouldn't drive off with her minivan. He had only said that he wouldn't leave her stranded. It could mean that once she had the driver of the sedan under control, he could speed away and leave her with that as her wheels. It would then be up to her to decide whether or not to leave the sedan's driver stranded as she drove off to follow him.

Common sense clicked in before that thought could rudely upset her equilibrium. He'd disabled the vehicle so knew it couldn't go anywhere. If he drove away, she would certainly be left stranded, which he'd promised not to do. The door of the minivan opened and curtailed this somewhat circuitous logic. She relaxed when he walked calmly to the back, opened the rear door, and sat half-in and half-out to watch the action. He gave her a little wave that she wasn't sure how to interpret.

She turned away, continued to the sedan, and held her gun to her side not facing the highway. It wouldn't do to alarm any concerned citizens who might be driving past but she wanted to make it obvious to whoever was behind the wheel that if anyone would fire the first shot, it would be her.

The driver was indeed the same young woman she had watched drive slowly past her near the Noir but she didn't look like she was about to open fire anytime soon. She was much more focused on the conversation she was having on her cell and looked like someone who was pissed off because an AAA dispatcher had told her that it might be more than an hour before a tow truck would arrive.

When she reached the car, she scanned the back seat and saw no one laying low and ready to leap out in an ambush. With her gun, she motioned the driver out. The young woman ended her call and complied.

Agony scrutinized her thoroughly. She was about a decade younger than herself, her brown hair pulled back in a ponytail that ended below her shoulders, and was dressed in an off-the-rack pants suit—comfortable and practical but it wouldn't win any style awards. She flipped the woman's jacket and found no signs of a weapon or a holster and took a step back.

"I need to see a badge," she stated.

"I haven't had a badge since I grew too old for the Girl Scouts." The young woman seemed to be trying her best to combine snarky with confident but her delivery didn't quite live up to her intentions.

"Oh, good." The ice in her voice managed to convey everything the driver's voice had failed to deliver. "Neither do I so I guess that makes us almost equals."

"Look…" The woman fidgeted. "My backup will be here any minute."

"Huh." Agony almost felt sorry for her. "Someone with no badge has backup? So what were you doing at the Noir? Planning a girls' night out but when you saw the commotion decided to find somewhere else to spend the evening? You should have all stayed in the same car. That way, you wouldn't have to try to contact the other gals to explain to them why you might be late. I seriously doubt that they will

44

hop into their Toyotas and rush to your rescue anytime soon."

"You have no idea who you are dealing with." The woman was certainly trying her best to summon some bluster.

"And apparently, neither do you."

"I *do* have backup, and they *will* be here at any minute."

No badge but backup. At least one of those statements was a lie and she was fairly certain that it was the latter.

"All the more reason, then"—she moved a step closer—"for me to make this quick."

"Listen, bitch, if you—" Agony's strike was so fast that blood spurted out of the woman's nose before she even realized a punch had been thrown. The pain managed to pass the information to her brain and she clutched her nose and cursed while she tried to staunch the blood flow with the sleeve of her suit jacket that would probably never be suitable to wear in public again. Bloodstains could be a bitch to get out.

"Manners," she chided and put the hand holding the gun into the pocket of her coat. The visual of the weapon had served its purpose and it was obvious by now that no one would draw a weapon. "Bitch I may be," she said coldly and decided to give her a brief lesson in proper etiquette, "but it is very rude to point that out while we're still in the getting to know one another stage."

As the woman focused on stemming the tide of blood that seemed determined to vacate her nasal passages with as much haste as possible, Agony chanced a glance at Bertha—her pet name for her minivan.

She had named the soccer-mom-mobile after the Jimmie Castor song, "The Bertha Butt Boogie" and had always found its beat irresistible. Even though the song stated that Bertha Butt only had three sisters—Betty Butt, Bella Butt, and Bathsheba Butt —she had often wished that she had had enough of a booty to shake to make the ground quake and had adopted herself into the Butt Sisters Family. She would often bop along or more than once, cruise along a few notches above the posted speed limit and pat Bertha's dashboard as she told her, "Keep rollin', Bertha. Two of the Butt Sisters are on the job."

Pain had found the bottle of wiper-fluid and the roll of paper towels she always kept in the back. He now had the middle seat folded flat and was in the process of wiping the outside of the compost-smelling case that held his gear. At least he hadn't hopped in the front seat to do this, and Bertha would smell much better once she climbed behind the wheel again.

"Who are you?" Agony turned her focus to the woman whose nose had finally stopped bleeding. "And what do you want?"

The girl pinched her nose between her finger and thumb as she answered, "I work for the government and you are in big trouble."

It came out as, "I worb bor de gobbermen an you are in bib prubble," but she was able to decipher it well enough.

"Oh, little girl." She took another half-step forward. "That's barely a quarter of an answer." The driver took a half-step back. "Nasal passages aside, no one says government like that unless they mean federal. So my question is which of the initials does your branch go by? Oh, and as far as me being in big trouble, I think I was about five years old the last time I wasn't in any trouble at all. As I grew, the trouble got bigger. So, which alphabet agency do you work for?"

The woman had finally staunched the blood flow and removed her hand from her nose but remained silent. Agony flexed her shoulders again as if in preparation to deliver the next punch. Whatever federal agency the gal worked for, she was more afraid of them than she was of any more blows she might receive.

"Okay, I get it." She cut her a little slack. After all, she had once been a young woman herself and had to work through the ranks. "Why were you tailing us and what do you want?"

No answer was forthcoming but the woman's gaze darted to

Pain, who seemed to be ignoring them as he continued to wipe his case fastidiously.

"Hhmmm." She realized that she seemed to be third on the list of the people the young agent was fearful of, even though she carried a gun that was easily accessible. Since the feds—who were first on the list—were not available at the moment, she decided to nudge her toward the man who was second on her list and was currently preoccupied with holding a very dangerous-looking roll of paper towels.

Intent on his cleaning, he didn't seem to even notice their presence.

"Let's go." Agony nodded toward Bertha's butt-end. The young woman now had a deer in the headlights look and she truly began to feel sorry for her. Not enough to offer to pay for her dry-cleaning bill but still, at least a little sympathy had crept in. Along with it was an awareness that they had been in one location for way too long and it was time to finish this little road-side drama and move on.

"Look…" She sounded like she was talking to her younger self who was home late from a curfew but had to either step inside the door and face the music or spend the rest of her life sleeping on the front porch, afraid of ever entering the house again. "If I shoot you, the big scary man will rush over here and grill me on why I had to pump lead into you. He and I will get into a big argument about how dangerous you seemed to be and the imminent threat I thought you posed that led me to believe I didn't have any choice. Or you and I can walk over and have a chat with him like the strong, professional, competent women we are."

"Do you promise you won't let him shoot me?"

"I can't even promise that I won't shoot you myself." All sense of sisterhood had vanished from her tone.

Pain was satisfied that he had cleaned the stench from his case the best he could and debated whether to keep the used paper towels in the back of the minivan to be disposed of in the next acceptable trash container they came across, or to toss them to the side of the road. The latter would provide job security for the county debris-cleaning crews so it was tempting.

It had been a long time since he had seen anyone being frog-marched, but by golly, that was exactly how it looked as the Bitch, now known as Agony, compelled the sedan driver to approach.

He knew she must have forced the scared young agent to face him at gunpoint, her weapon now held in one of her coat pockets. *Damn, she wears a long coat well.* The sedan driver stopped five feet in front of him as his newly acquired partner took four steps sideways and leaned against a guard rail.

In all honesty, he had to admire her action. They hadn't known each other long enough to build anything resembling a bond of trust and she had positioned herself so she had a clean line of sight if she had to shoot. The first person in that clean line was the female agent. If she went down or moved in any way, he would be directly in the line of fire without Agony having to adjust her aim.

The truth, he realized, was that with the proper aim, she could eliminate both of them with one shot, the first target a through-and-through of the female's neck with the round ending up somewhere between his dark-brown eyes.

For some reason, that realization made him smile—one that made the female agent's knees begin to shake even more than they had been. And yes, he knew she was an agent who was, at that very moment, trying to decide who she feared the most. He wondered if that was the same look he had worn as a young agent when an operation suddenly went sideways.

Pain tossed the gal his roll of paper towels and deliberately aimed it low enough that she had to bend to catch it. This gave Agony a clear shot at his head without placing the young woman in the bullet's flight path.

She didn't take the shot but she did point at her wrist as if she wore a watch and wanted to indicate that time was ticking away.

"The paper towels," he informed the agent, "are to help you to try to soak up some of whatever blood decides to flow. How much do you know?"

"Enough," she admitted.

He nodded at that confirmation and thought that the agents kept getting younger every year. It was easier than to admit to himself that he was getting older every year. He preferred to think the agency was beginning to recruit high-schoolers, even though his various aches and pains reminded him that the assumption was probably nothing more than wishful thinking on his part.

"Enough." He sighed. "So they know I am back in the country." It was more of a statement than a question.

"They sent me to track you, didn't they?"

"They should have given you more training before they sent you out on your own." He felt sorry for her when he suddenly realized how expendable they thought she was. The same thought dawned behind the young girl's eyes. To her credit, she threw the roll of paper towels to him and straightened.

He caught it and flung it behind him into the minivan in one swift movement while his gaze never left her face. Her expression was one he'd seen before and he recalled a safe place they could head to once this situation was resolved.

Agony watched the scene unfold from her perch against the guardrail.

"Obviously," the man she knew as Macarena Pain said, "SISTER doesn't seem interested in minding her own business."

"So it would seem." The woman's voice finally held neither fear nor smarminess.

"Then please." He made a request, not a plea. "Pass this message along. If they stay out of my way long enough for me to finish the Quest, I promise to be on my best behavior with her agents."

"This?" The woman held her bloodied sleeve out. "You consider this your best behavior?"

Pain chuckled and nodded toward Agony, who was still firmly rooted to her position at the guardrail. "I never laid a hand on you. The lady over there runs her own show. She is merely my ride for the moment."

He leaned closer and whispered into the young agent's ear. "Someday, if you live long enough, you might find another agent you can completely trust. Stay righteous. They can never take righteousness away from you, no matter how hard they try."

Without waiting for a response, he looked past her to Agony and nodded. "I'm ready to go when you are, ma'am."

She frowned. The only thing the roadside episode had established was that the woman and whoever had sent her were after Pain, so she was no closer to knowing who had put the hit out on her. She gestured for the young woman to return to her sedan to wait for either her backup or Triple-A to arrive.

Pain closed the back door and moved to the passenger seat, as his companion—with a glance back to make sure the woman wouldn't pull a bazooka out her ass—climbed behind the wheel. She drove for a while in silence and put as much distance between her and the stranded sedan as quickly as possible while they both remained alert for any more trailing vehicles.

Finally satisfied that they were in the clear, she broke the silence.

"Okay, even though I am merely your ride." She put enough heat in her voice to make it clear that she was less than pleased with that designated role. "I still think you owe me an explanation of what the fuck that was all about."

"Owe?" He hadn't mastered the raised eyebrow as well as she had but he could hold his own.

"Yes, owe," she insisted. "Before you appeared out of nowhere,

I was on a simple missing persons gig and making peace with Gus so I could work in his territory without having to watch my back at every second."

"Oh, yes," he interrupted. "I remember how well that was working out for you."

"Okay," she admitted, "I may have over-estimated his level of cooperation but now, I smell federal-grade bullshit with a capital F. The onus for that escalation is on you, my friend. Will you talk or should I simply pull over and let you try to hitch a ride with the first person willing to pick up a large danger-stranger with a thumb out?"

"Fair enough." He punctuated the words with a half-smile. "Explanation forthcoming in the not too distant future. But first, I suppose I should live up to my last promise to you."

"Remind me again what that was."

"Seeing and meeting our little tag-along back there reminded me of something. Keep heading north. I think I know a place where we can go to ground—at least temporarily."

CHAPTER SIX

Pain recited an address from memory and Agony punched it into her GPS and watched the route map out.

"Why did you tell me to head north?" She was curious. "Our new destination is five miles south of where we started inside the Noir."

"Habit." He shrugged. "I always head north when I don't have a specific destination in mind. You never know how long it might take to decide and Canada always seems like a good option. If I can't think of something by the time I get there, I might as well keep driving. There's a city there I've wanted to go back to for a couple of decades now. Have you ever been to Canada? Or to Gander?" He smiled wistfully. "Man, I love that city."

"No. I never have." The fact was that she had never been in any country whose name didn't begin with United and end with America. But having been raised in the city, she had learned that all she had to do was travel a few blocks in any given direction and she would find herself in a neighborhood that didn't require a passport to feel as though she had traveled to another country altogether.

"I've never heard of Gander." She thought she had the name

right. "Toronto, Montreal, Quebec, yes, but where the fuck is Gander? It sounds like one of those cities near the Canadian Rockies that specializes in ski slopes." She was making polite chit-chat while she found a turn-around and headed south again.

"The Rockies? No." It was hard to tell what the look in his eyes meant. "It's in New Foundland on the east coast. I was there for three days once when I was a teenager. I've always wanted to make a return visit."

"You fell in love with a city you only spent three days in? It must have been one hell of a three days."

"It was. I was flying back from a summer work-study program in England but our flight was redirected and we had to make an emergency stop-over, so the plane landed in Gander."

She chuckled. "A plane full of high-schoolers? I assume they put you all up at a hotel and it was suddenly party time, huh?"

His eyes were unreadable now. "There wasn't enough hotel space available. The whole town only had eleven thousand residents, so it's not like they had a ton of hotels."

"Not even enough to accommodate one planeful?"

"Thirty-eight planes landed that day, carrying almost seven thousand passengers. The town's population practically doubled overnight. All the locals opened their doors to take the stranded passengers in."

Agony laughed, "Are you sure you spent your work-study summer in England and not in Amsterdam? When the hell did all this take place?"

He looked out the window and fixed his gaze on the skyline. "September eleventh, two-thousand and one."

"Oh…"

"I spent three days in the home of Mr. and Mrs. Everett Adams. Whenever I think too hard about death, destruction, and chaos, I try to picture their honest, open faces that held nothing but kindness."

She remembered where she had been that day and drove on in silence, letting the solemnity of the memory have its due.

"So tell me," Pain said a few minutes later. He decided that since he had been the one who caused the moments of reverent silence, he now had the obligation to break it. Besides, they still had another twenty minutes before they arrived at their destination. "Since you are not a soccer mom, why choose such a stylish mode of transportation?"

"Sometimes," she replied with a smile, "one has to choose practicality over style. I could have driven my Fiat today but where would you have tossed your gear? Or would you have simply tie-wrapped it onto the back fender and let it bounce along behind us?" She patted the dashboard. "Besides, Bertha and me are like sisters."

He leaned back against his window and gave her body a quick once-over before he shook his head. "Sorry, I don't see it."

"Don't see what?"

"Enough of a butt for you to be one of the Butt Sisters."

She might end up putting one right between his eyes, but it wouldn't be for his lack of musical taste. For now, she decided to keep her focus on following the blue line on the GPS until it eventually informed her that, "Your destination is on your left."

Agony parked, stepped out of Bertha, and stared across the street at the outside of the Imperial Palace.

"A massage parlor?" She couldn't keep the incredulity out of her voice. "Our safe place is a massage parlor? Maybe you missed the memo, pal, but hiding out somewhere that the boys in blue might raid at any moment is not my idea of safe right now."

"There is simply no pleasing you, is there?"

Pain retrieved his gear case and circled the vehicle while she made sure to press the locks and set the alarm, hoping her wheels would still have wheels when she returned.

"You're bringing your gear in?"

"Do you honestly think it would be safe if I left it in Bertha?"

In her cop days—or any other days for that matter—vice was one thing. Sex trafficking fell into an entirely different arena. Hookers and johns. Escorts and their dates. She had made her busts on the merry-go-round as required and tried to keep her moral judgments to herself. Everyone had needs but she had no mercy for the pimps.

Some of them haunted the bus and train stations with a keen eye out for the runaways or the star-struck prom queens who "just knew" their path to real fame was in the city. They would promise to help find their dreams in the big city while they hooked them on drugs and used them for as long as they could still turn a profit before they abandoned them on the street.

But the massage parlor pimps, who posed as legitimate business owners, had begun to proliferate and had set up what could only be labeled as sex trafficking rings. She couldn't even guess at the deals and promises that had been made as the destitute families on the other side of the Pacific sent their children off with promises of a better life waiting for them on the opposite shore.

The better life ending up with them having to pay their debts off in ways that the girls' families back home had never imagined.

Agony trailed a step behind as Pain entered through the Imperial Palace doors as if it were a second home. She couldn't help the instinct to catalog every warning sign that it catered to more than merely the need for a good sweat or some knock-off version of a shiatsu massage. Honestly, she expected to see a menu posted on the wall listing their daily massage offerings with a note that stated, *Happy ending specials change daily. Please ask manager for pricing details.*

"Stop looking like a cop," he muttered. They stood in the lobby and waited for the attractive woman at the front counter to finish with a phone call during which she had a schedule book open to check available dates and times.

"I'm simply standing here," she snapped in response. "And I'm not a cop—at least not anymore."

"Tell your eyes that." He kept his voice low but firm. "You were born with cop's eyes and you'll probably die with cop's eyes. Maybe you should invest in a stylish pair of sunglasses."

After the brief but intense exchange, his voice took on an oddly sympathetic tone that she hadn't heard him use before. "I bet you were a good one."

"One of the best," she answered and sounded neither prideful nor apologetic, although the tightening in her chest reminded her of the solid feel of her detective's badge—one she was no longer allowed to carry, especially since she'd had to surrender it when she'd left the force.

They lapsed into silence. Pain knew where they were and what awaited them, while she took everything in and looked for any nuance she might have missed. The hostess behind the counter, while still on the phone, looked up and smiled as she held up a just-one-minute finger.

She couldn't stop herself from thinking that she saw dollar signs in the woman's eyes. *A couple,* she heard her think. *There are always big profits from couples.*

Another young woman appeared from the back, pulled out a stack of papers from under the counter, and held them up for the hostess to see. The woman gave the papers a cursory glance and nodded, and the worker returned to the back rooms.

Try as she might, Agony couldn't see any signs of distress in either of the women and wondered if she had become too jaded and saw mistreatment where none existed. The neighborhood might have been a tad on the dicey side and the décor choices needed serious updating but hell, that could also describe ninety percent of the neighborhood diners and bars her comrades in blue would often frequent.

"Nice place," she muttered distractedly.

"It's a nice place to visit," Pain replied with a smile that was impossible to interpret, "but I wouldn't want to live here."

She wasn't sure what had surprised her more—the fact that she had spoken her assessment out loud or his response.

The hostess was still on the phone and penciled notes into the scheduling book when a middle-aged man appeared from the back room. He was of East-Asian descent, that much was clear, but she would have stepped away from any bet that tried to narrow down which countries or islands he had drawn his heritage from.

At several inches shorter than she was, it placed him around five-foot-seven, which was roughly nine inches shorter than Pain. The man was also razor-thin and that contrast with her companion's muscular appearance was also almost frighteningly obvious. He was also impeccably dressed, another attribute that he and the other man did not share.

Agony had a flash-visual in her head that the larger man could pick him up, snap him over his knee, and break him in half should the ensuing conversation not go his way.

"Gotong," the newcomer said with a slight bow of his head and not a trace of fear in his voice.

"Bora." Pain mirrored the head-bow as he replied. With no obvious bodily contortions on his part, it seemed to her that he and their host had no size difference between them.

After her recent encounter with Gus, she worried that a gun might be drawn at any moment. She also knew her current partner didn't do guns, so she kept a hand in her jacket pocket. If she suddenly had to draw her weapon, she wanted to be ready. She watched for a couple of seconds as the two men faced one another and neither of them moved a muscle.

She had never heard Gotong and Bora. For all she knew, those two words could mean "fuck you" and "fuck you too, asshole." She had become fairly fluid with the Camorra's greetings to each other when meetings were about to begin but other than that, her linguistic experiences were rather limited.

She frowned when the two men suddenly embraced each

other. Pain took a step back and motioned to her as he kept an arm around the shoulders of the thin man.

"Bora," he said, "I would like to introduce you to my friend... ummm..." He took another step back when he realized that he hadn't learned her real name yet, and he started the introductions over.

"Hey, new friend." He winked at her. "This is my old friend, Bora. He calls me Gotong. I have no idea what that means although I suspect it is not a compliment."

Observing their body language, Agony had no doubt that Pain knew exactly what it meant and if she had to make a guess, she would have gone with ass-wad. She smiled because only good friends could insult each other that way.

She took a step forward and following the ritual she'd witnessed, inclined her head slightly before she took a half-step back.

"My name," she said and held her hand out, not forsaking western culture completely, "is Alicia Goni."

Habit almost added, "private investigator," but this introduction was about names, not current or past employment records. She was more than a little surprised when Bora took her hand in both of his and kissed the back of it.

"Ahh, Alicia. Such an easy-flowing name. I hope, someday, to welcome you more properly."

He smiled at her and released her hand before he returned his focus to her companion.

"Ahjoomenoni is unavailable at this moment, but I will let him know that you have returned and seek his company. Although I must warn you that he has still not forgiven you for having toppled his king with only two pawns."

"Please remind him," Pain said with a sharp nod, "that he is the one who left his knight exposed."

"I think, perhaps, that I will leave that reminder for you to deliver." Bora smiled. "Your room has been untouched since you left it. I assume that is why you are here?"

"Yes, Bora, you assume correctly, as always."

Agony kept her cop's eyes open and her mouth shut as she followed them. Her partner winked at her as if to say, "wait until you see this," and held his case in front of him as he proceeded.

Their host led them to a side door and down a steep flight of stairs to a basement. The room was clean but she wondered about the number of boxes that were stacked almost to the ceiling to leave only a couple of narrow walkways between them. Bora wound through these and eventually, moved one stack of boxes deftly to the side to reveal a utility panel.

At least I know where the fuse switches are if the lights suddenly go out. When he pressed the panel, it popped open to reveal another door and another set of stairs going down.

He patted Pain's stomach. "It is a good thing you still have no paunch, Gotong. Otherwise, I might need a crowbar to un-wedge you should you find the way too narrow and became stuck."

There were no lights on the narrow staircase but still trailing behind, she knew that if she lost her footing, she wouldn't fall too far before her way was blocked by Pain. When they reached the subbasement, Bora flicked a light on and her companion ducked as he passed through the door. She entered and realized that he had, at the most, two inches of clearance between his head and the ceiling.

While not spacious, the room was still larger than she had expected. There were two cots on opposite walls, a small table, a couple of stainless steel chairs, and wire shelving anchored to the far wall. Two doors led out of the room, one of which was open enough to see the shine of an old but not too badly stained toilet.

"I will leave you now." Bora bowed. "And I will let hjoomenoni know that you have returned."

"Thank you." Pain returned the bow and the thin man ⸎arted up the stairs.

Agony had a little more time to examine their surroundings now and was slightly taken aback by a floor drain in the middle of the room. The drain didn't surprise her but a fair amount of discoloration on the floor looked as if blood had been washed down the drain before a cleaning agent and elbow grease were applied to address the stains.

She also noted that one of the steel chairs showed scuffs, scratches, and even a dent or two along its arms and legs. These suggested that handcuffs might have been used as well as duct tape and a zip-tie or two that had to be cut off.

Instinct made her slide her hand into her coat pocket that held her pistol. He noticed the move and gave her a quizzical look.

"You can't blame a girl for being too cautious."

He nodded. "Maybe we should sit and talk, Alicia."

"It's Agony. No one calls me Alicia and lives except for the gentleman who welcomed us. It's rude to kill a host, at least at the first time you meet them."

She nodded toward the chair that held all the markings of having been used for interrogation, torture, or—with a couple more modifications—electric shock treatments. "You take that one."

CHAPTER SEVEN

Pain took the indicated seat and stretched his legs out. "Where do you want to begin?"

Agony kept one hand in her pocket with the trusty S & W but wasn't sure if she wanted to sit or wander around to inspect what was in the boxes on the shelves. She chose to sit for now.

"Let's start with names. You now know mine but I have my doubts that your first name is Macarena."

"And why do you doubt that? Maybe my parents were big Latin dance-pop fans."

"Because the song came out in 1993 and I estimate that your coming-out party was a few years earlier."

"Damn, I am beginning to look my age, aren't I?"

"And besides," she pointed out, "Macarena is a girl's name."

"Good point."

"What if my ring tone had been 'The Bertha Butt Boogie?' Would you have given me Bertha as your first name?"

"Not a chance."

"And why is that?"

"Because Bertha begins with a B. I always go with an M because that is my first initial."

"And what does the M stand for?"

"Moody. Which is why I keep changing it, depending on how I feel at any given moment."

"Okay, so you intend to remain coy about your first name. How about your last name? Pain. How close to the truth is that?"

"Extremely close. Spot on, in fact, depending on how you spell it. P-a-i-n, P-a-y-n-e, or P-a-n-e... Damn, I'll have to check my birth certificate before I can give a definitive answer."

Agony stood. Her curiosity about what was stored on the shelves had gotten the better of her. "I notice that your shirt has more than a few bullet holes in it. I would ask how they got there but since I was present, I know. Kevlar?"

"Kevlar is so old school."

"So no body shots if I want to stop you?"

"It would be a waste of good bullets."

She had thought they were simple boxes on the shelves but they were all solid cases, each one with a combination lock built-in. She slid a couple halfway off the shelf, enough to feel the weight inside.

"I assume these aren't filled with Girl Scout cookies?"

"Chopped up pieces of Girl Scouts, maybe, but no. No cookies."

Agony hauled one box down and placed it on the floor. She stepped back, drew her gun, and aimed at the lock. Even the best combination locks could be beaten by a few rounds placed dead center.

"I wouldn't advise that." Her companion sounded calm but there was a note of concern in his voice.

"Oh? And why is that?"

"All the cases are bulletproof and we are in a confined space. Bullets ricochet somewhere and if you plan to shoot me, I would prefer a direct hit, not some randomly lucky bounce."

She placed the case on its end and used it for a seat as she pulled the magazine out of her S & W and counted the cartridges.

He thought it was an interesting power move on her part. She didn't aim the gun directly at him but reminded him that it was ever-present.

"The girl from the beige sedan. She was obviously after you and not me. Do you care to fill me in?"

"The ones who put a hit out on you. Do you care to fill me in on that?"

"I asked first."

"That you did." He heaved an extended sigh. "What the hell. We'll probably never see each other again, so why not? You used to be a cop, right?"

"Emphasis on the used to be." She nodded regretfully.

"And I used to work for the good old US of A."

"Let me guess. Postal worker?"

"I wish it were that simple. Look, I was—or maybe still am, although no one has sent me a paycheck lately—an operative for a redacted branch of American intelligence."

"You're with the CIA?" She could almost believe it, except he now acted on American soil so that didn't seem quite right.

"No. And for what it's worth, I think the initials for that agency should be CYA—Cover Your Ass—and leave intelligence completely out of the equation. But I was in a whole different sub-section. One that has mostly been redacted."

"And what did your...uh, sub-section do?"

"We started as both covert and overt support in various theaters around the globe and provided assistance for a wide scattering of American military operations. Eventually, we ended up wherever we were sent, whether we had an established military presence there or not, and did what we were required to do."

He wasn't sure he wanted to explain any further and was saved, at least temporarily, by Bora's voice over speakers she hadn't noticed.

"Gotong and friend Alicia. It is getting late and Kwan's will be closing soon. We are going to place an order. Shall I put you down for a Bibimpap Pizza?"

Agony had no trouble interpreting the light in Pain's eyes when he answered.

"If you do not put me down for one," he spoke to the air, "then not only will I write you out of my will but I will also not name my firstborn child after you."

"A namesake would be nice, but I do not anticipate that happy event happening any time soon," the man retorted. "The reading of your will, however, I always expect to be on the immediate horizon. I believe that if you divide your estate up equally amongst all your friends, my share should come out to two dollars and ten cents, and I would regret having to miss out on that financial windfall. I will have it delivered when it arrives."

"Two dollars and ten cents for each of your friends?" She wasn't sure what to make of that last statement. "How many friends do you have?"

"I was never good at math." Pain shrugged. "How many is twenty bucks divided by two-ten?"

It wasn't the tone in his voice that made her reassess his physical features. Maybe it was the close quarters and the lighting, but she suddenly realized that despite his large frame and musculature features, his face was very gaunt and it might have been a while since he'd had a good meal. And hey, who could ever argue with a pizza?

She finished fiddling with her gun and placed it in her pocket as she returned to her questions.

"I heard you and your friend mention something about a sister? Is this anyone I might know?"

Pain was tempted to revert to his initial moniker for her because the Bitch seemed to never run out of questions. He decided he might as well get it all out.

"We were talking about a department known as the Strategic Interventions for the Securing and Transporting of Expunged

Resources. S-I-S-T-E-R. SISTER. Those in the know often refer to her as Big Sister, Big Brother's evil twin."

"But in the book, Big Brother was evil."

"In real life, he is a sweetheart when compared to his sister."

"And how does SISTER come into play here?"

He couldn't get into any more trouble than he already was. "SISTER is responsible for tracking and removing any operatives, current or past, who the government needs to expunge for whatever reason, leaving no trace that the operatives ever existed."

Agony let that sink in for a couple of moments before she suddenly stood from the case she had sat on and made it clear that she now had her gun grasped firmly inside her coat pocket.

"Operatives who need to be expunged. Like those who might have gone rogue or worse yet, traitors?"

Pain understood her sudden suspicions and didn't take offense. "There are many reasons why an operative might fall out of favor with the higher-ups, exactly like there are multiple reasons why someone who was once a 'best' cop might now have a price on her head."

She removed her hand from her gun pocket, shrugged out of her long coat, and draped it over the case she had vacated before she settled her ass in the steel chair opposite him.

"I believe," she said finally, "that the only appropriate response to that remark is touché."

He nodded at her peace offering.

"So," she went on, "I suspect your story doesn't have a happy ending but I would like to hear it."

"Damn. How long does it take to get a pizza delivered?"

"Will you keep stalling or do I have to go for my gun again?"

With a sigh, he stopped stalling and not because he had ever been in fear of her gun. "In my case, as simplistic as it sounds, it was a simple clerical error."

"That's one hell of a paperwork blunder."

"The agency had just gone through a change of leadership at the same time that a South American regime had a change in dictatorships. The new leader was no friend of Uncle Sam's and we—meaning my partner and I—should have been instructed to extract ourselves immediately. Let's say the message didn't get passed through to us in a timely manner and we landed in a situation that was not in our favor."

Agony was glad that she'd shed her coat. She was sweating enough simply listening.

"We identified two means of escape and decided to split up, and each took a separate path. Our thinking was that at least one of us had to get back to report what had happened. By splitting up, we thought we had a better chance of not getting caught in the same trap and that at least one of us might get through. One of us did and one of us didn't, but before I could give my report, the agency decided it was much simpler to expunge both our names and records than to explain our government's snafu in that shit for weeds republic."

"And that's where SISTER came in?"

"And where she remains. Damn. I'm getting hungry. You?"

She let him get away with that deflection. He had done an admirable job of acting sanguine as if the whole episode had been merely another day at the office, but she could tell that it was a façade he no longer wanted to maintain.

"I'm fucking starving," she answered and realized that she wasn't lying. "Oh, and by the way, what is on a Bimiminiara Pizza?"

"Bibimpap," he corrected her as the subbasement door opened and Bora appeared.

"Where shall I put it?"

Pain pulled a case off a shelf and positioned it on the floor between himself and Agony. The other man put the box down, along with a paper bag of utensils and napkins. "I told Kwan that it was for you and a guest. One half is spiced to your tastes." He looked at Alicia and smiled. "Perhaps you might be advised to dine from the side that he does not."

With that, he retreated, glad that Gotong had a dinner companion to share the delight with.

He knew he had to let the pizza cool for a spell before he could even open the box so he decided to throw in a few questions of his own.

"I showed you mine so it's your turn to show me yours, Ms. Best Cop."

The pizza smelled wonderful but she decided to return the courtesy of history-sharing and began with some hesitation. At least he was a man who could understand.

"I had a partner once—hell, working up through the force, I had any number of partners. Some were good and others simply drank their way through long enough to be able to collect a pension. But when I made detective, I got a good one. Noah Merckowitz." She smiled at the memory. "We called him Merk and he wasn't only a partner. He was my mentor and for three years, he taught me everything I never knew I didn't know and treated me with way more respect than anyone else in the force ever had."

"I'm sorry." She could see the sympathy in his eyes.

"Sorry for what?"

"For your loss. He sounds like one of the good ones."

"He was and he still is." She laughed. "He took full retirement at sixty-two and has been living out his dream down in Belize aboard his boat with his new partner, Raphael. Each day, they take tourists out to explore the wonders of snorkeling in the largest reef this side of Australia's Great Barrier and is having the time of his life."

He looked confused. In the short time she'd known him, she had never seen him look confused before and realized that she had been distracted by her sweet memory.

"When Merk retired, I was assigned a new partner. His name

was Alejandro Infante and his nickname on the force was All-In. The man had a motor that never stopped. I called him Alex."

Pain understood. "All-In is the one you lost?"

Agony nodded at his question that was not a question at all.

"We were deep into an investigation—one of those assignments that can either make or break a career—and we were close. We were so damn close. We had called it a day and headed home. I made it to mine but Alex didn't make it to his."

Oh, yeah, Pain knew exactly where she was coming from.

"Instead of doubling down on the case with more manpower, I was given a new case to handle and the investigation was shuffled away as if it had never happened. I pressed and got nothing but pushback. Then I pressed some more and ended up shouting down a self-righteous supervisor in front of the whole squad room."

"I assume he didn't take too kindly to that?"

Agony stood and pantomimed the motions.

"He shouted in response and got right up in my face as he dressed me down for not trusting his command, so I broke his nose—bam, right there in front of God and everyone. It was the best punch I've ever thrown." She sat again. "And the last action I ever took as a cop."

"Badge and weapon time, huh?"

She nodded. "My union rep worked miracles to get me out with at least a partial pension instead of jail time for assaulting an officer. It was one of those backroom deals. I was kicked off the force so I couldn't hang around to draw every eye I could to whatever shady shit surrounded my partner's death and they got to continue to sweep everything under the rug."

"So you took the deal?"

"I had assaulted an officer and there was a whole squad room as witnesses, so I was looking at a very good chance of prison. It's hard to continue trying to dig the truth up from behind bars, and Alex and the family he left behind deserve the truth."

"I hope they get it." Pain was sincere. "Both for their sake and yours."

He couldn't hold off any longer and opened the box from Kwan's. There it was, the almost delicate rice baked between two thin sheets of buttered dough and sliced into eight square pieces. Kwan had thrown in at least five different dipping sauces.

"Forgive my rudeness but one of us has to eat something or keel over."

"Help yourself but don't take the last bite."

The truth was that although she was starving, she wasn't quite sure of the proper way to eat the concoction. She decided to wait and follow his example so stalled for time.

"Tell me about this Quest of yours."

Pain held a finger up to indicate that he wouldn't say anything until he had savored his first bite. He dipped his square in one of the sauces, closed his eyes, and moaned with pleasure. Ignoring her, he dipped it into a different sauce and seemed to find it equally pleasing. Finally, he wiped his mouth with one of the paper napkins that had been provided and took the time to answer before he took a second square.

"It's not important to anyone but me and I don't make it a habit to put my problems on other people if I can help it."

"Then what was with that whole 'wait here, I need to get my gear crap' all about?"

He smirked as he tried to decide which sauce to try next "I did say if I can help it."

Her phone buzzed—not "The Macarena" so he guessed it was a text. He was proven right when she read through a series of them quickly before she looked up.

"I need to respond to these. It won't take a minute."

She read through them again. They had all been from Jamal, a thirty-year-old nurse who lived across the hall in her apartment building and who, she suspected, had a crush on her that began the day he'd first moved in a year earlier.

The police had arrived and when they didn't find her, they began knocking on doors. They'd told him he must contact them if he saw her come home.

Are you in trouble? Anything I can do? was his last text.

I'm always in trouble. She added a smiley face. *Nothing serious. Thanx for letting me know. Will talk when home.*

"If you intend to stay here for any length of time," Pain advised her between bites, "you'll have to ditch the phone. We can't afford to have anyone track you here."

"I hear you," she responded and basically ignored him.

Instead of turning the device off, she began to scroll with an intensity that was almost frightening.

Agony had remembered the young gangster's phone that she had accessed, cloned the data from, and sent it to her private cloud server. Now, she pulled it up and rushed through porn and dating apps while she vaguely noticed how many dating profiles the young buck had set up for himself. *Funny,* she thought as she glanced at one of them, *he didn't look like a dentist.*

After a moment, she pumped her fist, then repeated the gesture—a sure sign that she must have found something.

"Yes!" she shouted.

"Do you care to share?" he asked.

"Sure," she snarked. "It's a to-die-for recipe for cannoli. Sorry." She looked up and smiled apologetically. "It concerns my missing person gig, which probably seems like small potatoes to someone like you."

She put the phone away and nodded toward the pizza. "May I?"

"Kwan would be offended if you didn't."

With more caution than was probably necessary, she picked a piece up, dipped it in a mild sauce, and hesitantly took a bite. She made the first piece all-gone in thirty seconds.

"Your missing person may be small potatoes to me," he said as they devoured the rest of the bibimbap, "but not to those who are missing him. Tell me more, please."

"Sure," she conceded, "but stop me if it gets boring. It's important to me and I don't want it to be trivialized."

"Deal."

Agony summarized as if laying a case out to a lieutenant along with why she thought it was worth pursuing. The man was a member of the Nigerian community who had gone missing almost a week earlier. Rumor had it that the police considered him a person of interest in the death of another Nigerian national who had worked with him as a delivery driver for a local warehouse.

"I was first contacted by an elder in their local church—one of those storefront affairs with a small but devoted congregation, and the missing man was their minister. Elder Misoungo told me that they not only hope I can find him but that I can also clear his name from any suspicion."

"If he's already been gone for a week, it sounds like two very tall orders." Pain tried to be both realistic and sympathetic. He did not envy her the task. "So what was with the fist pumps?"

"The reason I went to see Zaza was that during my initial information-gathering stage in the community, I suspected that some members of the Nigerian gangs might have been involved in the death of the co-worker. I'd also heard rumors that some of Zaza's younger boys had reached out to the Nigerians, looking for a way to undercut the Columbians and especially when it came to heroin, which is one of the Nigerians' specialties."

"And that was something you wanted to get in the middle of?" He already knew she was tough but he hadn't taken her for being stupid. "Do you have a death wish I don't know about? Because now would be a good time to tell me."

She shook her head. "It is because I don't have a death wish that I went to see Zaza. I wanted to let him know that I was working on a very singularly focused case and that none of it involved him and the Camorra activities."

"Except for maybe the drug-running part," he countered, "which makes up ninety-eight percent of their business."

"I would have eventually explained how inconsequential my inquiries would be but was distracted when the guns were drawn. Oh, and thank you, by the way, for having saved my life."

"Twice," he reminded her.

"Fine." She almost pouted. "Twice."

"You're welcome." The thanks were a little late in coming but he accepted them with a fair amount of grace. "You still haven't explained the fist-pumping."

"Oh, that." She tried to shrug it off. "I got lucky. During all the fun, I managed to snatch a phone up and transferred its data to a private server. I will get rid of this phone soon as you suggested, but I found a whole series of stored texts and calls between Zaza's young dude and one he labeled as Afri-Ben. I'm hoping that Afri-Ben can give me one big fuck of a leg up on finding out more about the Nigerian gang and their connections to the missing minister."

Pain finished picking at the few crumbs left in the box from Kwan's and closed the top neatly.

"The cot behind me is mine. The cot behind you is yours. It's been a long day and it's too late to accomplish anything now. What do you say we start fresh tomorrow?"

"We?"

He smiled. "There may be some overlap in our worlds after all. Maybe I can tag along."

"I can't quite picture you as a tag-along kind of guy."

"Hey." He was offended. "When the occasion calls for it, I can remain perfectly discreet in the background of someone else's show."

"Yeah." She wasn't certain it was the right decision. "I've seen your version of discreet. But this is my show and I will need people to talk to me, so can we keep crashing through windows and head trauma routines to a minimum?"

"Here I am," he grumbled, "offering to help, and all I get from you is nit-pick after nit-pick after nit-pick."

"Oh, I haven't even begun to nit yet. You should see me knit." She smiled at her in-joke that he wouldn't understand at all.

CHAPTER EIGHT

The day before had been a long day's journey into night, and this one was shaping up as more of the same—hurry up and wait, which she hated. Tonio, whose phone she had copied at Zaza's, had arranged to meet Ben, the African, after a concert the Nigerian insisted on attending.

Agony and Pain were both surprised that the concert wasn't at one of the many secular venues in the city that featured live music at night. Instead, it was held at St. Alban's Cathedral and featured the Marambigueax Choir, which made their first tour of the United States. Their blend of Gospel spirituals set to African beats had been featured on NPR and St. Alban's was their third stop in what was proving to be a very successful introductory tour.

The performance began at seven pm and had been a complete sell-out. The partners had arrived early and staked out a parking space as soon as the metered parking ended at five pm. Like most cathedrals in the city, St. Albans had no parking lot per se. There was a small park across the street and a multi-level parking garage on the other side of it.

"I don't know why we couldn't have taken Bertha." She was

still a little annoyed. "There is more than enough room in the back. At least more than in this Buick."

"This has more trunk space."

Earlier that day, he had rummaged through one of the cases on the shelves in their subbasement abode and changed into a shirt that had no bullet holes in it. He had then disappeared for half an hour. She had used the thirty minutes to freshen up in the spartan but relatively clean bathroom.

When he returned, he'd flipped a set of car keys around his finger.

"How," she'd asked, "is tooling around town in a stolen vehicle any better than Bertha?"

"How do you know these aren't the keys to my car?"

"Are you saying they are?"

"I'm saying no one will say they aren't."

She had learned enough about him by that point to know to not engage in circular arguments.

Now, they sat in a large sedan her father might have been proud to drive. They had wanted to arrive early enough to be able to watch who entered the cathedral so they could mark off as many of the five hundred attendees as possible, which left them with time to kill before the cathedral started to empty.

During stakeouts, even with partners who knew each other well, chit-chat often ran out after the first half-hour. When you spent ten hours a day with someone on a daily basis, there wasn't much to catch up on. Since they didn't have a history to go on, the two fell into familiar patterns to pass the time while they waited for the shit to break loose.

"You're mumbling again," Agony pointed out.

"Sorry." Pain sounded almost apologetic. "Chaz and me used to play mental chess during recon and sniper ops. The main game was silence—days and days of silence while rolling over to piss in the weeds or the sand. If we had a flat surface, he would draw the board in the dirt with a blade and we would pass the blade between us to indicate our moves. I was going through the Four Knights."

"His name was Chaz?" She'd caught him out.

"Yeah," he confirmed with a sad smile. "About once in every dozen games, he'd let me beat him so he wouldn't be left playing alone while I pouted. Now, I play alone. You know how it is. What's with the crocheting?"

"It is knitting," she corrected him. "Crocheting only requires one needle. Knitting takes two."

"Well, mea culpa." He threw his hands up. "I guess your mother taught you more about it than mine ever taught me— which is understandable, what with you being a girl and all."

"I have killed people for less condescending statements," she responded without missing a stitch.

He let the silence have its turn while he counted. Eighty-seven stitches—or whatever the hell they were called—later she filled in the blank.

"Alex used to knit while we were on stakeouts. Before we became partners, he had been a pack-a-day smoker until his twins were born. He dropped the smokes cold turkey and picked up the needles. I was proud of him for that, you know? Wanting to live long enough to see your children grow up and then bounce grandchildren on your knees. He would knit things for his children but that didn't mean I wouldn't give him shit about it."

Once again, he understood. As a Go player, he had once told Chaz that chess was for pussies.

"You can't play Go in the sand," had been the reply. "Tic Tac Toe, maybe. Talk about a game for pussies."

"But come on, girl." Pain tried to bring them back into the moment. "You look like an Amish housewife."

"An Amish housewife," she countered, "seated in the front seat of a motorized vehicle? I don't think so."

She had him there.

"And?" He knew there was still a missing piece.

Agony drew a deep breath. "They cleaned his locker out. It was stuffed with balls of yarn and pictures of his *ninos* taped to the doors. After the funeral, I asked his widow if I could have the yarn. She asked me why and I told her that Alex had some unfinished work and that I would be honored if I could finish it for him. She let me have it and the twins graciously accepted my finished products. I specialize in scarves and hats and leave sweaters to the professionals."

"I assume you have reached the end of his yarn? Because otherwise, I don't know why you are blending purple, orange, blue, and brown."

"What? You don't like the color scheme?" She thought she had done a masterful job of blending the colors.

"Name me any sentient being who would?" Pain pitied anyone who would end up wearing it.

"I'm glad that's settled, then." Agony leaned back, still not missing a stitch as she looked at him. "You, not being a sentient being, will be able to wear this cap with pride. I only hope I have enough yarn left to cover that massively inane head of yours."

"You know…" He turned his head so that she could take in the whole circumference. "Sometimes, you gotta make do with what you have."

"Oh, fuck us!" She dropped the yarn and needles. "The concert's over!"

"How fast time passes." He knew he had at least forty-two smartass responses but decided this was not the time to share any of them.

From the front seat of the Buick, they watched as the assembled crowd headed out through the front doors of St. Alban's. Zaza's Tonio was not their focus, even if he had survived to attend the meeting. Afri-Ben was. Although five hundred people exited, they only needed to find one.

Agony pulled out the phone Pain had told her she had to get

rid of, pulled up an app she used to disguise her number, and called the number she had for African Ben like no telemarketer had ever used that trick before.

Damn twenty-first-century technology. Twenty-seven people were already talking on their cells and she had no idea which of them had just answered a call. She was about to hang up when Pain demanded her phone in the most expedient way possible. He simply snatched it out of her hand.

"Watch the crowd." He shouted the order with no time to explain. She didn't take the command graciously but complied while he waited for a few seconds and then shouted, *"Olly olly oxen free motherfucker Ben!"*

Only one man with a phone to his ear froze and he now had her undivided attention.

"Got him!" she reported as he made a sudden move that separated him from the crowd. "But Olly olly?" she asked her companion as a stream of obscenities could be heard as a reply through the phone. "Maybe you can give me a warning before you start screeching like a schoolgirl."

"I thought it was a very manly screech." He defended himself cheerfully.

"So would Howdy Doody, I'm sure!" She had no intention to let it go.

"Howdy Doody was a quality program, Miss Peanut Gallery." He wouldn't let it go either.

"Sure," she snapped because they were on a roll now, "if you like creepy-ass puppets who pre-dated the dinosaurs."

"He was a marionette, not a puppet!" Pain was mentally gearing up the same way she was. "Jim Henson would back me up on that."

Their fight paused when they realized that the Muppets might be the one thing that they had in common from their younger days and they had to give Jim Henson his due. When they looked at the scene again, Afri-Ben pocketed his cell and moved rapidly through the crowd, accompanied by two other men who had no compunction in shoving anyone out of their way as they hurried to a stylish SUV in a prime parking space about five car lengths ahead of them.

"I count Ben and two bodyguards," she observed, "but can't tell if they're armed or not."

Her partner had located the SUV and put the Buick in gear. "It shouldn't matter. Now, slap me across the face—hard enough to leave a mark."

Agony's MMA training didn't cover slapping so she struck out, punched his mouth, and split his lip.

"I said slap!" He pulled his hand from his mouth and saw blood.

"You said hard enough to leave a mark." She shrugged. "I can try again if you like."

"That's okay." He eased forward as Ben and his cohorts entered their SUV. "The blood will suffice."

Pain pulled out of their parking space and proceeded to swerve directly into the back door on the driver's side of the SUV.

"How could you do that?" he shouted in a nasal whine as he opened his door and climbed out.

She had hit him squarely in the mouth so she wasn't sure why his nasal passages should suddenly take prominence, but he left his door open and shouted loudly enough to be heard three blocks away.

"We have reservations in half an hour," he continued to whine. "How can I arrive like this? I might need to go to the hospital and that means I won't have any leftovers to take to our fur-babies, not to mention that the dog-sitter is charging forty dollars per hour. It will cost a fortune if I have to spend the night in the hospital."

Agony stepped out on her side of the Buick and circled the rear so that she could come up behind him. He continued to whine and seemed to shrink as he approached the driver of the SUV. His legs were no longer straight but slightly bent at the knees. Along with a slight hunch to his back and that curved his shoulders inward, he didn't look nearly as dangerous as she knew he was.

"You started it!" she shouted after him. "I don't care if you hate my mother or not. You should have never called her that."

Ben and his guards had jumped out of the SUV at the moment of impact and stood facing the pathetically whining man who approached. They seemed reassured that this was not a gang attack. It was merely a sissy-boy who had more woman on his hands than he knew how to handle. They had difficulty restraining their laughter.

"I'm sorry! I'm so, so sorry but she hit me." Pain pointed at Agony who approached rapidly. "She hit me while I was driving." He pointed at his bloodied lip as evidence.

"And now that you're not driving," Ben said in his lilting and rhythmic Nigerian accent, "I believe I will hit you for what you did to my ride."

"Oh," he pleaded, close enough for the Nigerian to be able to make good on his threat, "My insurance will cover that, no worries. But I'm not sure what the policy will cover with regard to your boys' faces."

"Say, huh?"

"The damage to his face." He pointed past the first bodyguard and toward the second. The silly kids had lined up side by side instead of one on each side of the man they were supposed to be protecting.

The closest turned to the one Pain pointed at so he never saw the punch launched at his ear. It burst the eardrum and caused an instant loss of balance that made him crumple.

The second guard tried to draw his gun but his hand didn't get near it as their attacker delivered one kick to the guard's arm and another one directly to the chest that hurled him against the SUV before he collapsed.

Ben moved his hand to his gun in his shoulder holster but Agony snapped her baton out and flashed forward to deliver a hard blow on his arm. His gun arm useless, he rushed her and was met with a sharp baton blow to his face. It wasn't hard enough to kill or knock him out but hard enough to break his nose and he clutched his face as his knees gave out.

Pain delivered a knee to the second guard's ribs that convinced him to stay down. He removed the guard's gun, looked at Agony, and frowned.

"It's always the face with you, isn't it?"

"He'll thank me later when he sees what an improvement it is."

"I thought you said no head trauma," he chided her.

"Tell that to your buddy's ear." She pointed at the guard who now had a trickle of blood dribbling down his neck. She made a quick search, snatched up the two remaining guns, and shoved them in her coat before she pointed at the Buick with her baton.

"Would you care to be chivalrous and load our catch up?"

"So now is the time you pull out the damsel in distress card?" He walked past her, prepared to duck, and reached the side door of the Buick. "I'll meet you halfway," he added, swept the door open, and bowed with a flourish. "Or would you prefer the trunk?"

"Trunk please, asshole. As long as we have one we might as well use it."

Pain popped the trunk and Agony twisted one of Afri-Ben's arms behind him and forced him to the rear of the vehicle. Her partner came to her assistance once she'd made use of a couple of zip-ties on their captive's wrists and ankles and he lifted the drug runner and dumped him, with a serious lack of consideration, into the cavernous space.

"We're beginning to draw some attention." She felt she should point that out.

He slammed the trunk shut and looked around. The whole time between the initial fender-bender and the trunk deposit had lasted less than two minutes, but that had been enough for a small crowd to have gathered. They stayed a safe distance away but he had no doubt that of the dozens of cell phones now taking photos, at least three of them had been used to call nine-one-one.

"It's time to boogie." He hurried to take his place behind the wheel as she slid into the shotgun seat.

"You do realize," she said as he accelerated away, "that at least a dozen phones will have pictures of the license plate to show the cops when they arrive."

With a smirk, he shrugged the concern away. "Good thing it's not my license plate."

"Oh. So you admit that this isn't your car?"

"I didn't say that." He cut through an alley. "I said it's not my license plate."

CHAPTER NINE

Pain made a few more turns than Agony thought necessary to get out of the St. Alban's area and slowed what she'd hoped would be a speedy getaway. She used the time to wipe the blood off of her snap-baton before she stowed it in her coat.

Her annoyance grew a little more when he made a quick stop and without any explanation, hopped out and disappeared behind the Buick and out of her mirror range. He returned thirty seconds later looking pleased with himself and headed out again.

"Do you care to enlighten me?"

"It was a beige Buick. Do you know how hard those are to find these days?"

"I don't have an exact estimate handy, but I bet if you pulled to the curb, I could step out and see at least one."

"Yes," he nodded, "and it would be a fairly distinctive model so easily identified, especially if there was now a city-wide BOLO put out on one. The cops will find one with the matching license plate parked two blocks behind us."

He finally made a turn that took them to the quickest route to the Imperial Palace.

Agony forgave him for his dawdling during the escape. As a

former cop, she knew that if a BOLO went out on a certain make and model with a specific license plate, the first thing an officer would do if they saw one would be to run the plate before they pulled it over.

Pain had not only switched license plates but he'd switched theirs with one from an identical car. If any enterprising officer saw them and ran the plate, they would discover which type of vehicle that plate was supposed to be on. If the hit came up that it belonged to a Subaru, they would have a reason to pull them over. That was no longer a concern.

On the way to the Imperial Palace, she checked the weapons she had confiscated. There were three guns, all with no rounds fired. Out of the corner of her eye, she noticed her partner clench the steering wheel a little tighter than necessary. Remembering his aversion to firearms, she stowed them out of sight and as his shoulders relaxed, his grasp on the wheel lightened and he began to hum, his lips moving ever so slightly.

Her personal jury was still out regarding men or women who hummed. Him mumbling chess moves was one thing but humming?

"Shall I find a song on the radio you can sing along to?" she asked. "Or do you prefer a one-man karaoke?"

"I'm trying to remember Bertha's sisters' names." He looked at her with a smile and began in a soft baritone, "Bum, bum, bumadum... Bum, bum, bumadum... Betha Butt, bum, bum, bumadum."

"Betty Butt," she said as he maintained the rhythm with his bum, bum, bumadums.

"Bella Butt." It took her a minute to think of that.

"Bum, bum, bumadum," he continued and tapped the steering wheel to the rhythm. "Bum, bum, bumadum."

"Shit!" She almost had it—some Old Testament name. "Keep going," she commanded "It'll come to me but I have to start with the first."

"Bum, bum, bumadum," he supplied.

"Bertha Butt!"

"Bum, bum, bumadum."

"Betty Butt!"

"Bum, bum, bumadum."

"Bella Butt!"

Shit, she thought, *if the fourth sister's name was any closer to the tip of my tongue I could have bitten it off and spat it out.*

"Bum, bum, bumadum...Bum bum..."

"Bathsheba Butt!"

"Bum, bum, bumadum."

They looked at each other, high-fived, and finished in unison.

"The Butt Sisters!"

The impromptu singalong had no sooner ended when they arrived and parked in front of the Imperial Palace.

They exited the Buick. Agony glanced around and was relieved to find that her Bertha had remained untouched. She moved to the trunk and was shocked when Pain asked her for the drug runner's gun.

"You aren't a gun guy," she reminded him.

"Yeah," he answered with a wink, "but he doesn't know that. I'll play the bad to your good, all the way to the basement."

She dug in her coat and pulled out Afri-Ben's snub-nosed pistol. He popped the trunk and held it between the captive's eyes before he had a chance to shout and hope for a rescue.

With a wink at her, Pain leaned into the trunk and whispered in the softest, most threatening voice she had ever heard.

"I wanted to pump a bullet in your brain and dump your body in the river half an hour ago." He nodded at her. "But this lady wanted to ask you a few questions first. Do you understand?"

The question was answered by a terrified nod.

"Good." His voice was calm and soft as he explained. "What will happen now is that we will take you to a place where she can ask her questions and you can give her some honest answers. Simple questions. Honest answers. Understand?"

Another nod followed, which was not easy to do with a barrel against your forehead but Ben managed it.

"My only problem"—he continued his patient explanation of the situation—"is that if you answer correctly, we will probably let you live, but no one likes a tattle-tale. I can't let you see where you are in case you eventually decide to take revenge on your soon-to-be hosts."

With that statement, he ripped a strip of duct tape off and slapped it across the man's eyes.

"If it were up to me," he added and leaned even closer, "I would have stuck a fork in each of your eyes. But her majesty here has a kinder heart than I do and convinced me that it would be a cruel thing to do. She didn't convince me that you didn't deserve it but I gave in to her this time."

"What can I say?" Agony leaned into the trunk and sliced the zip-ties off. "I'm a softy that way."

"I will now pick you up." Pain delivered his last instructions in the same chilled tone. "I'll carry you in as if you were a wounded comrade. All you have to do is keep your mouth shut. Otherwise, your next cry for help will be the last words to come out of your mouth before I slice your tongue off and put a bullet from your gun through your brain. Please nod if you understand."

Ben nodded desperately and his tormentor turned to Agony. "I think we're good to go now. Would you be so kind as to get the doors?"

He lifted the Nigerian out of the trunk and cradled him in his arms as he turned toward the Imperial Palace. She slammed the trunk closed and focused on the doors ahead.

A moment later, she held the front door open and he carried the terrified man in. The woman behind the counter glanced up and down again as if she were in the middle of an advanced-level Sudoku puzzle.

Agony headed to the door that led to the first basement level and held it open and her partner repositioned the drug runner to hold him vertically upside down as he made his way down the stairs.

"This part is a little narrow," he advised the captive after Ben had put up a slight struggle while upside down and bumped his head against a wall.

At that point, the man went limp. He had probably reached the point of all hope lost and was praying for his end to be swift and not torturous. They reached the basement level and Pain stepped aside with his bundle so that she could open the door to the subbasement.

Once in the sub-level, he plunked the Nigerian onto the guest chair and zip-tied his wrists to the steel arms. He added another zip-tie around his ankles before he stepped back and let her take over. This was, after all, her gig.

"Ben?" Agony said calmly. "Would you like to see where you now are?"

"I am in the room where you will die," he responded and they both had to admire his spunk given a most unexpected circumstance.

Pain moved swiftly and yanked off the duct tape that covered his eyes, taking most of his eyebrows with it.

"Shit! Fuck—die, bitch!" the captive hollered.

"Try getting a bikini wax." She kept her voice steady. "Then get back to me about pain."

She sat on the box across from him and waited for his eyes to adjust to his surroundings before she continued.

"You only have one friend in this room," she informed him calmly, "and that is me."

Ben was fairly certain that he didn't have any friends in the room, but tried to focus on the woman who had busted his nose and not on the big man who wandered around and looked at boxes lined up on the shelves.

"All I need from you," Agony went on, "is some information."

"Then you can kill me now." The captive tried to sound brave. "I assume you traced me through my communications with Tonio so must want information about them. I know nothing about Zaza and Tonio's operations or how they distribute the drugs. I am only a potential supplier—nothing more than a salesman."

She met Pain's eyes at that admission. They had the right guy.

"What do you think?" The big man pulled two large plastic bottles out of a case on the shelves and held them up. "Will it take one or two bottles of bleach to clean the floor after he bleeds all over it?"

Ben's eyes suddenly noticed the drain in the middle of the floor in front of his chair and the stains that surrounded it.

"Oh, nice job, partner." She turned to him. "Now we'll also need the blue bottle to clean the urine up."

The Nigerian's bladder had loosed a yellow river that ran down his pants leg and onto the floor toward the drain.

"Sorry." Pain took a step back to observe her in action as the good cop.

She leaned forward in her chair and addressed the prisoner in an earnest voice.

"Neither I"—she nodded toward her partner—"nor he gives two shits about the drugs. That's between you and Zaza. We are only interested in finding a friend who has gone missing."

It was hard for Ben to believe that these two had any friends.

"Does this friend have a name?" He prayed it was one he had never heard.

"Doro," she answered. "It means Gift of God."

If the Nigerian had any bravado left in his body, it deserted him at the mention of that name but he answered gamely, "I know no man named Doro."

Agony leaned back. "Then I am afraid we made a mistake and you are no use to me. But you have admitted to being a drug runner so I will let the man who hates drug runners take over from here."

He saw the big man holding the bottles of bleach smile.

"I'll wait upstairs," she said as she rose. "Let me know when you are done with the body."

"Wait. Wait!" Ben would do anything to not be left alone with the man. "What name did you say?"

She sat slowly "Doro. It means—"

"Gift of God." The Nigerian nodded. "Yes. Yes. The preacher! I remember now."

Pain looked disappointed and set the bottles of bleach on the shelves as he waited.

"He was a minister, yes." Agony nodded encouragingly. "He was also a delivery driver. In which capacity did you know him?"

"I do not know him. I never met him."

She sighed. "Then once again, you are of no use to me." She turned to her partner. "Probably two bottles."

"If it was blood, yeah, you'd probably be right. He does look like a bleeder." The large man sounded bored as he retrieved a funnel. "But I hate to waste good bleach. I think half a bottle down his throat should do it."

"No, no! It's true. I never met him but I know what happened. If I talk will you let me live?"

"Life holds no promises," Agony informed him, "except that if I leave you alone with him"—she gestured to Pain—"you will most certainly die. At least with me, you might have a chance to walk out of here depending on what you say."

"I hate it when you do that." Her partner rummaged in another box on the shelf and withdrew a set of wristbands connected to wires that led to a small electrical box. *This is interesting,* she thought as she watched him strap the bands onto Ben's wrists before he handed her the box.

"It's not quite a lie detector, per se," he explained. "It doesn't have all those needles and gauges that put out squiggly lines when a lie is told so you'll have to use your judgment. But what it does have is this little red button you can push if you think he's fibbing."

He pushed the button and Ben's body went into a series of quick and painful convulsions. When the prisoner settled, he moved to stand beside the shelves next to the bottles of bleach and the funnel.

"I'm sorry." Agony looked at him. "You said the red button?"

"Yes, the red button. If you push the green button, I am afraid you won't be able to ask him any more questions—ever. And the smell of fried flesh can take days to clear."

She examined the little box, always careful to make sure she understood whatever weapon she held. With a small frown, she pressed the red button and Ben's body convulsed again.

"Got it." She looked pleased. "Red button, good. Green button, bad."

"Green would be bad for him." Pain nodded. "But I won't feel a thing so go ahead and knock yourself out."

Agony turned to face Ben, whose dark skin now had a touch of paleness to it.

"Okay." She began her interrogation, "I don't have the time to play twenty questions so, Bennie, Mr. Illicit Pharmaceutical Sales Representative, what can you tell me about the minister named Doro. Let's start with is he still alive?"

"He was still alive...the last I heard." The man expected another shock but she held off on the red button, even though his answer was less reassuring than she'd hoped for.

"Start earlier in the story." She needed to hear the whole narrative. "How and why did Doro go missing? And why is he being framed for the murder of a co-worker?"

"I never met him."

Agony pressed the red button and Ben convulsed again. She looked at Pain.

"It's only forty-eight volts." He answered the unspoken question in her look. "Unless he has a bad ticker, you can push the button for hours—but don't hold it down for too long at a time."

She liked that answer and gave the Nigerian the time to get over the latest shock before she continued.

"You have already told me that you never met him," Agony continued her interrogation calmly. "And I believe you. Now, tell me what you know about those who have met him and please, for the love of all things holy, don't mention your drug-running connection with Zaza's gang." She nodded at the big man again. "That might be of interest to Mr. Bleach over there, but I am the one with a finger poised between the red and the green buttons. That means I am the one you should try to make happy."

"But you might not be happy with my answers."

"True," she acknowledged, "but I need answers. Whether they are happy answers or not, I understand that you are not responsible for what happened to Doro so you will not be punished for that. But you will be punished for lying."

Pain had to admire her technique. She had made no promises she could not keep. Nor did she promise poor Ben a happy ending.

Internally, he smiled. Forty-eight volts was barely enough to give anyone anything other than a mild shock, unless the recipient stood in a puddle of water or in this case, sat in a chair, his feet surrounded by a pool of his wet piss. Water and electricity made a wonderful pair when it came to amplifying levels of pain felt when the red button was pushed.

A large metal bucket stood in a corner of the room. He had often used it to place a subject's feet in. Fill the bucket with water, press the red button, and bama-jama, out came the truth. But Agony was doing fine without that knowledge.

"Your choice, Ben," she said. "I can press the green button now and put you out of your pain forever. Or you can answer my questions and I promise that you will not have to deal with Mr. Bleach afterward."

Damn, Pain thought, *she made a promise that might be hard for her to keep.*

The prisoner looked from the bitch to the bastard and decided to go with the bitch.

"I deal with drugs—only drugs." He spoke directly to her. "All businesses are set up that way with separate departments."

Ben's body convulsed again when her finger slipped and pressed the red button again.

She turned to Pain. "I could get used to this."

"There ought to be an APP." He smiled.

"Whoops." Agony began again after Ben's convulsions stopped. "I didn't ask you for advice on how to delineate departments. I asked you about Doro. And in case you haven't noticed by now, I have been known to have a one-track mind. Tell me what you know about Doro."

Afri-Ben was a high-living, drug-running go-between, but he had heard stories and was ready to share.

"There is a gang—a group?—a something that is not a part of us. They deal in terrorism. The preacher and his co-worker had drawn their attention."

"In what way?" she asked as Ben focused on the big man readying a bottle of bleach and a funnel.

Both Pain and Agony knew that truth was about to be spoken, so with a minimum of questions, they let him tell it as best he could while facing electrical shocks and bottles of bleach.

Doro the preacher and a co-worker were nothing more than delivery drivers who made twice-weekly deliveries to a water treatment facility the whole city depended on. As drivers, they were inconsequential, but their knowledge of the treatment facility and how it was run was something that couldn't be learned from studying blueprints of the plant. The terrorist gang had to learn about the daily ins and outs of the facility's activities.

"So where do you come in?" She posed the question, not sure that she wanted to hear the answer.

"These terrorists approached our bosses. They promised money if we let them do what they needed to do." Neither of them could detect a lie in the statement.

"And what did they need to do?" Her heart dropped as she asked the question.

"They needed to take the two delivery drivers and ask them questions about the water plant and how it operated. The preacher and the other driver were both Nigerians and the other driver was a member of the preacher's church. The terrorists needed to know how, when, and where to take them both captive."

"And?"

"I don't know the answer to that." Ben hung his head and braced himself for another shock that didn't come.

"And?" Agony repeated her question.

"They were both taken together." He looked up and faced her with nothing but the truth in his eyes. "I don't know the whole story. All I know is that the friend resisted and tried to give the preacher a chance to run. He was shot for his efforts."

"And?" She gave the scared man a chance to continue with the narrative.

The Nigerian looked directly into her eyes. "And the terrorists...maybe—what is the other word?"

"Anarchists?" Pain suggested before he added, "Assholes?"

Ben looked at the big man and nodded. Anarchists was a term he was not familiar with but he could understand assholes.

"The assholes..." He continued his narrative of what he had overheard. "They shot the preacher's friend and left his body on the sidewalk."

He looked frantically left and right, hoping that at least one of the two believed him because, for maybe the third time in his recent memory, he had told the truth.

"Black-on-black crime," Agony said as she looked at Pain.

"Gang violence," he replied.

"Fucking useless immigrants," she responded.

"Film at eleven." He shook his head. "Shit, what an easy story to bury."

As tempted as he was to approach Ben with a bottle of bleach in one hand and a funnel in the other—for intimidation purposes only—his partner had made some serious headway playing the good cop.

She leaned forward and made eye contact with the man strapped to the metal chair, the Zap-box still in her hands.

"Please," she said, "finish the story. I need to know what happened to the preacher."

"These people still have him. They need to know how the water plant works day to day."

"They intend to poison the city's water supply?" She shivered at that possibility.

"No, no," Ben answered. "They don't have enough poison for that. And this is only what I overheard." He was fresh out of friends. "If you fuck with the filtration system, no one will know where or what has been fucked with."

"And who will know," Pain added from the background, "what water will be safe to drink or shower in."

The Nigerian nodded vigorously. "They—and with all the angels as my witnesses, I don't know who they are—don't plan to poison anyone. They only want the authorities to know that they can."

"Oh…" The large man couldn't help himself. "Who needs God on your side as a witness when you have twelve angels standing at the ready to take the jury box?"

"Huh?" Agony had to ask as Ben nodded at her question.

"Sorry." He apologized. "Not all angels are on God's side."

She shook that question off and made a mental note to save it for a rainy day before she focused on Ben.

"My only concern is Doro." She was ready to push the red

button so many times that her thumb would wear out. "Do you know where he is?"

"I know where he might be," the captive answered with an expression that said he expected more pain. He provided the details and waited while she dug for her phone to record them before she sat again. "But I can't guarantee that he is still alive."

"And why is that?" She held her thumb above both the red and the green buttons.

"Because…" Ben knew his end was near. "If the preacher tells them what they need to know, he will no longer be of any use to them."

"And if he doesn't tell them?" Agony knew the answer before she even asked the question.

"Same thing." The drug runner shrugged and prepared for the electrical shock that would end his life.

What he hadn't been prepared for was a kick to his chest from the big man that broke half his ribs as he and the chair toppled before his head thumped painfully on the floor.

Agony looked up. "Was that necessary?"

"Probably not." Pain defended his action blithely. "But I thought he would prefer it to a funnel of bleach forced down his throat."

"Oh, great." She glowered at him. "Now is the time you decide to go all logical on me?"

"It seemed like as good a time as any. Are you hungry?"

CHAPTER TEN

Pain had wanted to use the bleach to put Ben out of his misery and dump the body. Agony didn't want more death than was absolutely necessary and had argued against that idea.

She had wanted to take Bertha. He didn't want her soccer-mom-mobile to suffer any more damage than was absolutely necessary and had argued against that idea.

A compromise had been reached and they were now in the Buick and parked in the middle of a gang territory that was not on friendly terms with the Nigerians.

He popped the trunk and she assisted Ben, who was missing most of his eyebrows, cradled his broken ribs, and whose pants smelled of urine out of the trunk. They stood back and watched as he got his bearings.

"This is Kavyette Territory."

"That is correct," Agony confirmed. "If you are quiet and careful—and lucky—you have at least half a chance to make it out alive and get back to more friendly surroundings."

"You should have killed me in the basement."

"Why should we have all the fun?" Pain asked. "We're not the selfish types. Good luck."

The Nigerian scowled as the two climbed into their car and drove away. At least they had left him on a street beneath a streetlight that was not currently functioning. He looked up and down the street, realized to his relief that it was mostly dark, and hurried into the deeper shadows. With no ride, no phone, and no gun, the odds were not in his favor, but he wasn't dead. He began the slow, careful, almost hopeless process of trying to sneak out of Kavyette Territory alive.

Pain drove them towards the address Ben had provided as his best guess as to where the preacher was being held. Agony had been right. It would take the man hours to get out of the rival gang's territory so that should give them enough time to do what they had to do before the Nigerian had a chance to contact anyone to warn them.

As he drove, his partner tried her hand at chit-chat.

"How exactly does your Quest connect with my missing minister gig? And who calls anything a quest these days?"

"I do." He wasn't sure why his terminology seemed to be such a sticking point with her.

"What are you? Some kind of a knight of the realm or some shit like that?"

"I'm more like a pawn in someone else's game. But if I were a knight, would that make you a virginal damsel in distress?"

"I still have more guns on me than you currently do," she reminded him. "And I am more than willing to pull all of them out if you put damsel, virginal, and me in the same sentence ever again."

"Sorry, me lady." He inclined his head in a mocking bow. "But who the hell calls a missing person's case a gig? Do you have a band hidden inside your coat somewhere that you haven't introduced me to yet?"

"No, Sir Jerksalot," she sniped in return. "The band is hanging out and practicing two rooms down from the local RPG Club. Do you want to swing by for introductions?"

"Maybe another time."

Agony watched him drive and wondered if there was ever a time that his gaze focused solely on what was in front as opposed to scanning every mirror as if he expected danger to come at them from every possible angle.

"Maybe you should drive a convertible," she suggested.

"My hair is never long enough for me to enjoy the feel of the breeze flowing through it," he responded. "So I'm not sure what the purpose of a convertible would be."

"The purpose," she elaborated, "would be so that you could also keep an eye out on the sky for an aerial attack."

"A convertible?" He gave it some thought. "Probably not...but a sunroof might come in handy. I'll be sure to add that the next time I update my vehicular specifications request."

"All right, then." She looked out her window at the neighborhoods they were driving through. He seemed to prefer streets to freeways. "I have a missing minister and you have a Quest. I don't know the secret handshake of the Knights Templar but are you at least allowed to tell me why you think the two gigs might be related?"

"Are you familiar with the Black Ax confraternity?"

She also kept her eyes on the mirrors as she answered. "I don't even know what a confraternity is. And a Black Ax? What is it? A band of lumberjacks that uses Paul Bunyon as their password?"

"I wish it were that simple." Pain sighed and drove on. "The Black Ax is a Nigerian confraternity and some of their members are rumored to have connections with seriously bad people."

"How bad?" This was all new territory for her.

"Our mutual friend Gus and the Camorra?" She nodded. "They are like children sneaking in after a construction crew has finished their work for the day to scribble their names into a still-wet sidewalk and scamper off, laughing because they left their mark."

"Let me guess..." She thought he was being a little overly

dramatic but played along. "These bad people would be those who would have mixed Gus' people in with the concrete before they poured it?"

"Something like that, yes." Agony was chilled by the tone and truthfulness his voice conveyed. "These bad people leave no trace. They don't want anyone to know they even exist."

"I'm listening."

"I knew that some of Zaza's punks had reached out to the Nigerians as new potential suppliers for their heroin. They all swim in the same poisonous, murky-water pond. But somewhere above that pond is where my bad people dwell—like gods looking down from the top of Olympus, laughing at the antics of the mortals."

"You must be a real hoot at cocktail parties."

"I have my moments." He smiled but it faded quickly. "All I am trying to do is to find out which Nigerian fish has been hooked. That might at least give me a hint as to which line to follow out of the water to whoever is holding the pole."

"And are you any closer to that line now than you were two days ago?"

Pain took a breath, one deep enough that she wondered if his seatbelt might snap.

"No." He exhaled slowly.

"So why are you still sticking around to help me on my gig?"

"Can't I simply be a good guy who's trying to stay righteous?"

Agony looked wryly at him. "Sure, you could be. But your suit of armor has a few chinks in it."

"Damn." He looked at his clothes. "I hoped you wouldn't notice."

He took his eyes off the road and the mirrors for a brief moment and stated an unvarnished truth. "For purely selfish motives. I hoped that if I can help you save the preacher, maybe I could earn enough trust in the Nigerian community and something might shake loose that will lead me to my bad people."

"So you're piggybacking on my gig?" She tried to sound annoyed.

"Hey," Pain tried to sound conciliatory. "Neither of us was doing very well as a solo act."

"Fair enough," she acknowledged. "But you know way more about my gig than I do about your Quest."

They were close to their destination.

"Setting aside the archaic term, what is the point of any quest?" he asked in all earnestness.

"I don't know." Agony could die happy if she never heard the word quest again. "Slay a dragon? Rescue a princess? Find a holy grail? Try to buy off a volcano god by tossing glittery trinkets into its gaping lava-filled mouth before it spews?"

"Undoing evil," he said without a trace of embarrassment or equivocation. "That is what a quest is all about."

"Undoing evil? Seriously?" She was beginning to wonder if he was a sentimentalist or a former seminarian.

"I know that we can't undo the past," he continued, "but we can try to give evil a reason to pause."

"So, you believe there is such a thing as evil out there?" She had pondered the same question during more than one restless, sleepless night.

"I'll take my eyes off the road one more time," he told her, "if you can look straight into them and tell me that after all you have seen during your life and career, you don't believe the same thing."

"Keep your eyes on the road. I think we have a left turn coming up soon," she replied and withdrew from the conversation to make a pocket-check of her available weapons. It was easier to step back because nothing in her mental arsenal could argue his point.

Pain turned left, then right. They parked on the street in front of a small store in the middle of the block. At this hour, it was closed but signs hung in the window—*Fresh produce. Fresh meat. CBD and Kratom supplements arriving daily.*

"An interesting combination of goods," he observed as he read them.

"CBD and its uselessness," Agony commented. "Their producers have a great PR I'm aware of that. But what the fuck is Kratom?"

"Kratom," he informed her, "is the herbal equivalent of crack-cocaine. It is expensive, fast-acting, and will give you either a short energy boost, severe vomiting, or a painful case of constipation."

"Well, then…" She tried to envision the advertising campaign for such a diversified herbal supplement. "Put me on their e-mail list. Ben said that Doro was being held in the basement of the store's storage room the next door down. How about you pull around back?"

He studied the scene for a moment. The adjoining storefront was boarded up and shuttered. He guided the Buick around the corner and parked in the alley at the rear of the sealed building. They stepped out of the car and surveyed the back entrance—a metal door with a handle and a key slot.

"I got this," he informed her.

She stepped back and he produced a small putty-like compound and placed it in and around the lock.

"Do you have a light?" he turned and asked her.

"Do I look like I'm a smoker?"

"Fine. Make things difficult. But oh," he added, "good for you. Neither am I."

She shook her head when he pulled out a box of matches. Not a matchbook but an actual small box of wooden matches. He struck one and applied it to the end of a wick she hadn't seen him insert into the putty before he stepped back to join her.

"Shield your eyes," he advised.

The wick burned down until there was nothing much left of it to burn and she turned her head. She heard a quiet poof and felt a hand on her arm.

"The castle's basement has been breached, me lady," he said. "Shall we enter?"

"Add me lady," she informed him, "to the list of honorific titles that will precede your death the next time you refer to me by any of them."

"Fine, bitch." He shrugged and smiled. "You first or me?"

Agony turned to the door that now hung by a single hinge. The entrance to the storage room's basement was free for the breaching.

Did I just think breaching? She had to ask herself and then admitted that she had. *I may end up killing him after all. Breaching? What's next, forsooth?*

They approached slowly. Pain ripped the door off its remaining battered hinge and tossed it aside. The entrance led directly to a staircase to the basement. They heard music and possibly voices from below.

The plastic explosive had been quiet enough to not alert anyone that they had intruders, but it didn't mean that armed resistance wasn't in their immediate future if they descended the stairs into an unknown situation in which they would be sitting ducks.

She thought this would be the ideal time for her partner to draw a firearm that he had so clearly expressed an aversion to. Of course, he did no such thing and she smacked him on the back of his head as he started to take the first step down.

"What?" he protested as he spun to face her. "Do you want to do ladies first this time?"

"No," she retorted as she held out her backup gun, a snub-nosed S & W .38. "I want you to take this."

"The situation's not messy enough yet." He declined the proffered weapon.

"That's the point," she whispered, tempted to kick him down the stairs and let him draw all the fire. "You have it in advance in case things get messy."

"Don't worry about me." He dismissed her concerns airily. "I'm fine."

"I'm not worried about you, dumb ass," she snapped. "I'm worried about me having to save you."

"Oh." He smirked, "I so love role reversal games. I'll finally have a chance to play the virginal damsel."

"Not until you learn how to wear a floor-length dress while climbing down a flight of stairs. Have you had any practice with that lately?"

"Yes, but only in four-inch heels. My ankles wobble in anything higher."

The man was utterly exasperating. She sighed and let him lead the way while she remained two steps behind with two guns drawn, not sure if one of the bullets she might fire would be into the back of his brain.

The music and the voices continued as they proceeded cautiously, but they drew no gunfire.

Pain reached the floor and scanned the area before he stepped aside and waved her down.

She stopped beside him and saw the remains of a recent bloodbath.

The music came from a CD player. The voices came from a wall-mounted television screen. Bikini-clad bitches complained to each other about how their men didn't appreciate them.

Agony shot the living shit out of the TV screen while he found the power cord to the CD player and ripped it out of the electrical socket.

Silence fell and they studied the scene. They didn't have to worry about having to cover each other's flanks. The room had no doors or windows and no living bodies were left to attack them. The floor was strewn with nothing but bodies and blood.

Pain's attention was drawn to a spray-painted skull and crossbones on a wall. The paint was black and it was crude but distinctive.

Her attention was focused on looking through the bodies on the floor as she tried to determine if Doro was among them. She rolled them one by one. Her job wasn't to identify them all. That task would be left to the professionals who would eventually arrive and have to make some sense of the slaughter. She had to try to find one specific body.

"The tag," her partner said, "is from the Supreme Eiye but something isn't right."

She looked at him from her knees, her pants and sleeves now drenched in blood as she searched through the bodies. "Something isn't right? Tell me one thing about this whole fucking scene that is right."

"The Supreme Eiye and the Black Ax." He exhibited a singular focus as he looked at the tag on the wall. "They are rival Nigerian gangs but they don't need to leave any messages to each other after a deed is done. Neither of them would have needed to tag a scene like this."

"I found one still alive!" she shouted.

He spun as she was shoved aside by a small blood-covered woman who tried to scurry to the stairs. She scrambled after her, caught up to the woman, and wrapped her arms around from behind as they both writhed on the floor. The escapee struggled to free herself but Agony held her and made shushing sounds.

CHAPTER ELEVEN

Both had seen horrifying scenes before but the basement they were now in rivaled them all. The woman Agony held in her arms was either a participant in the bloodbath or a terrified victim. This was not the time to trust anyone.

"She's crying." His partner looked at Pain from her position on the floor as she held the small woman.

"The ability to cry on demand has earned many actors and actresses Oscars," he said as he approached cautiously and knelt beside them. "Cradle her," he instructed, "but don't give her a chance to pull out either a knife or a gun."

She understood the need for caution and nodded as he shifted a little closer.

"What is your name and why are you here?" he asked and the small body went limp.

"I am called Lucy," the quavering voice replied.

"I will sit up with her now," she told him quietly. "Ask away."

She eased Lucy with her. Pain had learned enough about his partner to be able to trust her instincts and sat on the floor so that they could all be at the same eye level.

"Lucy?" he began in his most gentle voice. "What happened here?"

The survivor looked first to the woman who had prevented her escape.

"He asked you a question." Her voice at the moment was nothing if not compassionate. "Please answer it."

The woman hung her head and avoided all eye contact. Agony glanced at Pain long enough to let him know that she thought the woman she held in her arms was truly scared. That was good enough for him.

"Lucy?" He used a gentle finger to raise the victim's head enough that she could see his eyes and repeated his question. "What happened here?"

She looked from one to the other and released her fears. The story she told was a painful one.

"My parents," she started, "own the store, and they use the third floor of this building for storage. A gang man come in and say they want to use the basement."

"How did he know about the basement?" He maintained eye contact.

"We hire many people. Everyone who ever worked for my parents knows about the basement. Poppa asked why they want it and was told it was none of his business but that his business might suffer damages if he didn't say yes."

"So he said yes?" He could imagine the gangster's play.

Lucy nodded. "He had no choice. They use the back door and we never see them anymore, except me."

Agony ran her hand softly over the girl's head, "Why did you see them again?"

"They need food, yes?" The woman turned so that she could look at her.

She nodded and Pain eased himself a few feet back.

"Everyone needs food," she agreed.

"They made me bring them food and water—and beer. I do that and they not hurt the store or my parents."

"How many were there?" She took over the questioning.

"Always four but not always the same four. Four gang men and the minister. Doro," she added. "His name was Doro. He was not here as a volunteer."

"He was a hostage?"

"Hostage, yes." Lucy nodded. "Like a prisoner. He needed food and water also, so I come twice a day and stay to make sure the holy man eats."

"Did Doro talk to you?" Agony hoped for more but the girl shook her head.

"Only the first time. He said it would be dangerous for me if I knew too much so after that, all he ever said was thank you."

She looked at the bodies, all of them Nigerian, and pointed at one. "He—Samuel—made sure other gang men leave me alone to serve food. I do not flirt but he said he liked my smile so at him I made sure to smile, but he scared me. One time he say he wants to see me after they are finished in the basement. For my family's safety, I pretend I like him too, maybe a little."

"You were very brave." Agony encouraged her with another stroke of her hair. "What happened tonight?"

"Early today they receive message that holy man must be moved, but they must wait for other men to come and take him. So all guards come for one last night together. I made much food. The music played and the television was on when I came down the stairs carrying the meals."

The partners remained silent as Lucy took the time she needed to face her memory.

"I set food on counter and served two dinners. I was carrying a plate for Samuel when people rush down the stairs with guns going off. The plate I was holding broke and I dive on the floor. Many guns. Samuel dropped on top of me. Blood—so much blood. I hold still and pray they think some of the blood was mine."

"Were any of the men who had rushed down shot?"

"Everyone was shot. I heard some of new gang men shout in pain." She looked around the room. "But I see none of their bodies here so they must not be killed. They grabbed the holy man, Doro. He was injured but could walk still and took him up the stairs. I could not see much from under Samuel but I saw one of the new men paint on the wall."

"Are you sure it was one of the new ones who painted?" Pain hadn't meant to interrupt but he needed to know. "How can you be sure?"

"The same way I am sure none of the new men died here. Only Nigerians are dead. No white men. White was the skin of the man who painted."

He hung his head and muttered, "I knew it. More obfuscation and misdirection."

After a moment, he put his strong hands on the young girl's shoulders and willed her to feel their strength in the hope that she could take some of that strength in as he faced her.

"Lucy? Look at me," he said with a gentleness that did not match his body so it had to come from somewhere deep within. Lucy looked up and met his eyes.

"You are very brave. You are very kind. Your parents will be very proud of you. Do you have a cell phone so that you can call them?"

The girl had to twist a little but pulled a cell from a back pocket and held it up.

"Good." He smiled. "We have to leave now. What you need to do is call nine-one-one, then call your parents. Tell them all what you told us."

"What should I tell them if they ask about you?"

Pain looked at Agony as they both tried to remember if they'd spoken each other's names out loud within her hearing. Thankfully, they hadn't.

"Tell them two strangers were having a quickie in the alley and stumbled down the stairs by accident and found you."

He knew he would get shit for that one but hey, you gotta get your jollies while you can.

With a serious scowl at him, Agony made sure that Lucy was out of the shock-stage and could dial. They rushed up the stairs and into the Buick.

"Which way is north?" he asked as he slid in behind the wheel.

"It truly is always north with you, isn't it?"

"It's never failed me yet."

"Go to the end of the alley and turn right."

Pain followed the suggestion and they were five blocks away before they heard the distant sound of sirens.

"Just so you know," she said, her displeasure biting in her tone, "I don't do quickies."

"Neither do I." He fixed his gaze on the road ahead on the assumption that it would make it harder for her to put a bullet between his eyes. "That's why it was such a perfect cover-line."

"Tell me," he asked after a moment, "if there is a flaw in my thinking."

"Oh, I can think of a hundred different flaws in your thinking and I've only known you for two days."

"I mean about the events that led up to tonight."

"I'm listening."

"We picked up Bennie the pants pisser but left a few of his boys still alive on the sidewalk. One of them managed to contact these new players to tell them that the preacher might need to be relocated. The new guys—who from what we know of them won't be pleased about the Nigerians having fucked up a simple assignment for the second time— decided to cut their losses and fetch the preacher themselves."

"Doro." Agony had developed the habit of repeating victims'

names. It helped her to remember that they weren't merely a statistic.

"Doro." He nodded in understanding. "But they knew that if they did that, they ran the risk of the Nigerians compromising their whole operation as a way to retaliate."

"The skull and crossbones tag was nothing more than a confusion diversion." She could see it now as clearly as Pain did. "They set the whole basement scene up as nothing more than gang rivalry."

"The Black Ax versus the Supreme Eiye." He was glad she hadn't found any flaws in his theory so far. "The two gangs will be so focused on each other that they will forget all about the—" He caught himself. "They will forget all about Doro."

"So where does that leave us?" Agony's brain was in high gear as she could see the pieces of the puzzle being laid out in front of them.

"Their target, Doro, is still alive but wounded." Pain sensed that the road they were traveling on was slanted and they were heading more north-east than north but decided to let it slide. "Also, we know that at least one of the tagger's gang is also wounded. You know the city better than I do. Can you think of any place they could head to for on-demand care? Somewhere that doesn't worry about having to report to the authorities when they treat gunshot wounds?"

She didn't have to wrack her brain too hard to come up with a best guess. "Maybe one."

"Shit," Pain said after an hour and a half of following Agony's directions as she read them from her phone's GPS. "I was hoping for a Waffle House."

"If you had only taken the freeways," she retorted, "instead of insisting on winding through the streets, we would have been there an hour ago. Breakfast will have to wait."

She had directed him to the Miles & Ignatius Funeral Home and Mortuary and he realized that eggs over-easy would not be on the menu, even if the sun was about to start its daily journey over the horizon. He circled the block.

"Your turn to spill," was all he said as the speedometer never moved a hair above five MPH.

Where to begin?

"Douglas Miles." She decided to go with the partner whose name came first on the establishment's stationary and sign. "He was once a trusted local pharmacist who ran his own store. His problems began when he started to sample his merchandise."

"I'm guessing he ended up losing his license?"

She nodded. "He lost his license but not all his connections to the under-the-counter suppliers he had built relationships with."

"And Iggy?"

"Jules Ignatius was once a well-respected medical examiner for the city. Miles' weakness was the pills. Iggy's weakness was the ponies."

"They sound like a charming duo." He couldn't come up with a better way to describe them. "And now Iggy serves as the mortician and Mr. Miles is what, the funeral director?"

Agony almost laughed at the image of Douglas Miles as the director of a funeral home. The last time she had seen him, he stood five-foot-seven by three feet wide and had nose hair that he could use as a mustache if he ever took the time to learn how to wax it properly and smooth the ends out.

"No one ever brings a dead body here. A body that isn't quite dead yet and needs patching up? Yes. And if Iggy fails to heal the body, the building out back is a crematorium. It saves on the cost of a casket and no one ever runs DNA tests on ashes."

Pain had finished circling the block and parked. "Mortician Trauma Care," he muttered and had to give the two their entrepreneurial spirits' due. "It puts a whole new spin on the old you stab 'em, we slab 'em routine."

"Are you done yet?" she asked as he put the Buick in park.

"Almost." He held a finger up as he considered other advertising campaigns. "You said there's a crematorium out back. How about you toast 'em, we roast 'em?"

Agony had to appreciate the man's way with words but that was a compliment she would save for another day. They sat in silence as they scanned the parking lot that held three cars before sunrise. None of them was a hearse or an ambulance. They had come to the right place. There were no lights on in the front rooms of the building but one room in the back threw out enough light to cast shadows on the trees.

"Your gig. Your call." He was ready to back up whatever play she made.

"Right through the front door." Agony had made her assessment and decision. "But let's not announce our arrival with any more fanfare than necessary."

"Have you ever heard how quiet a church mouse can be?"

Good God. He seriously might be a former seminarian.

Pain followed as she tried the front door and it opened without so much as a squeak.

She tried not to think about the bloodstains on her pants or the cleaning costs of the blood on her coat that she had acquired while cradling Lucy. She led him down a familiar hallway to a back room and paused outside the door. It was standard issue, solid on the bottom with a window on the top half that allowed them a view of the operating theater inside.

Agony didn't need to duck as she gazed through the window but she did. He looked over her shoulder. Someone he had to believe was Iggy worked with a scalpel on the leg of a wounded man lying on a table.

Another man, who did not appear to be wounded, stood to the side. He held a pistol in his hand and didn't seem to be able to stop himself from waving it around, although he always ended with it aimed at the so-called mortician's head.

Pain tapped Agony's shoulder and motioned her into the hallway.

"Iggy's the one with the scalpel?" He kept his voice low. She nodded and he continued to whisper. "I didn't see the preacher, did you?"

She shook her head and answered in her quietest voice. "No. I saw Iggy with a white boy on the table and another white boy standing guard without a steady bone in his body."

"Okay." Pain began to formulate their next plan of attack. "I'm glad we saw the same thing. You know you are covered in blood, right?"

"Me so bad." She looked at herself and then at him. "Does that mean our prom date has to be delayed while I go and change?"

"Nope," he assured her as he scooped her up and cradled her in his arms. "Be your natural charming young virginal damsel self."

Agony let loose with a stream of profanity she didn't know she was capable of as he kicked the door open and backed quickly into the room with a blood-soaked woman cradled in his arms.

"Got another one for you, Doc!" he shouted.

The terrorist who stood guard spun and shot him three times in the back before he delivered a back-kick that hurled his attacker into a table of medical instruments. As the clatter resounded in the tiled room, he dropped his bundle onto her feet and spun to assess the damage he had done.

It took only a moment for the terrorist guard to stumble to his feet, no longer holding a gun but with a set of surgical scissors protruding from the side of his neck.

"Don't!" Pain shouted as the man reached for the scissors.

"Don't what? Stab you to death with these?"

He yanked the scissors out of his neck and rushed at Pain as dark-red blood spurted from his carotid artery. His lunge wavered and he took one step forward before he collapsed.

Agony decided to hold off on her promise to shoot her partner for his virginal damsel remark and turned to face the doctor.

"Hey, Iggy," she said cheerfully. "Long time, no see. What'cha been up to lately?"

"Wishing your mother had come to me and asked for an abortion."

She didn't need help to deliver a roundhouse kick to his chest that catapulted him into a corner where he collapsed.

They turned their attention to the man who lay on a table with a bullet in his leg that hadn't yet been extracted.

"I have some basic medical training," Pain volunteered as he approached the table. "If you have some questions to ask, I will do my best to keep Mr. Dungheep here alive long enough to answer them."

Agony took him up on his offer and approached the table on the opposite side.

"I am looking for a preacher," she stated.

"Then maybe a church should be your starting point," the man managed to snap before he screamed.

"Sorry." Her partner looked across the table at her. "Bullets can be tricky things to extract and I might be a little rusty."

"Try not to kill him while trying to save him," she responded loudly enough for the patient to hear before she resumed her questioning. "I am looking for a preacher—a Nigerian. The bullet in your leg came from when you and your friends went to move him earlier tonight." She shook her head and remembered that dawn was about to break soon.

"Last night," she corrected herself, "you were sent for a preacher. Yes or no?"

The man heard her question and felt a slight nudge of the bullet still lodged in his leg.

"The African. Yes. I don't know why he's important. None of us know why. All we know is that the Nigerian has information."

"Information about what?" She kept her voice firm.

"How the fuck should I know? I do what I'm told."

Agony looked across the table and Pain nodded to confirm that the bullet was still lodged in the leg. So far, it wasn't causing too much discomfort as long as it wasn't nudged too much as it was extracted.

A couple more clumsy attempts and the offer of some pain pills from a bottle on a cart finally persuaded the man to talk. He assured them that he was only a foot soldier, after all, and grunts were never told anything more than they needed to know.

"The government is holding some political prisoners."

"You mean terrorists," Pain corrected.

"So says you. And we are part of a group helping to negotiate their release."

"Through the threat to the water supply?" Agony wanted to make sure the stories they had heard earlier matched.

"Yes…ow, shit! Pills…please!"

"Answers first." She took the bottle of pills from her partner and he continued his knifework.

"Only one prisoner matters. All the others are for cover."

"And why does this man matter?"

She wasn't sure if he would swoon from the pain or spit.

"He knows where a serious chemical weapon is hidden."

"Not the chemicals to poison the water? You are talking about an actual weapon?"

"Like a dirty bomb?" Pain gave the bullet a slight nudge.

"Yes, yes." He moaned. " Very dirty."

"So they are holding the minister to force him to help with their terrorist attack on the water plant." Something about this didn't pass her smell test. "In order to free a man who can help them plan an even bigger terrorist attack?"

"Yes." The man pleaded for the pills. "It's all being done for political reasons. I don't know what, though, okay?"

She looked across the table at her partner who gave his head a maybe-yes, maybe-no nod and elicited another painful scream.

"Look, the group I belong to started as radicals but we've moved on. Please, pills now and I'll tell you the rest of what I know."

Pain backed off with the scalpel. The man seemed in danger of passing out and this was not the time to have a witness go night-night. Agony shook some pills out and the man leaned up enough to dry-gulp them before he lowered his head and closed his eyes.

"We started with ideals and big plans. We were a dedicated group but small. It took a while, but we eventually learned the disappointment of not having enough funds and not enough believers or financial backers for our cause. But in our efforts to raise funds, we learned that there was good money to be made as terrorists for hire."

"And again, good old capitalism beats ideals." Pain shook his head.

"Our group came to the attention of another group who had deeper pockets. I don't know what they call themselves but they hired us to help pull off the main chemical attack. More pills, please."

Pain stopped Agony from offering any more. Instead, he held up the scalpel for the man to see.

"I will go back in for the bullet now but it is tricky because it is lodged next to your femoral artery. I suspect that you would prefer pain over death if my hand should slip? Which it is in danger of doing if you keep dancing around the truth. Do you understand?"

The man nodded and she resumed the questioning.

"We're running out of time and patience here. Wrap it up."

Her partner gave the bullet a slight nudge and drew another shriek.

"Things went sideways when one of the other groups got picked up. I think one of them was the leader of their cell. All I know is they are looking for the Captain—ugh—Budria!"

"Sorry," Pain apologized without an ounce of sincerity. "I almost had it."

"You said Captain?" Agony needed him to focus.

"I don't know what they call him but he would never have them hiding out with a prisoner in some abandoned factory that smells like bread mold and is overrun by rats. All I know is that I heard Captain and I heard Budria. I don't know if they are the same person or not."

Pain pulled the bullet out at the same time that the meds kicked in and the man lay still and mumbled himself into sleep. They had to lean close but they heard him say, "Rats won't matter much longer though. The cell has made their water threat and the city is willing to play ball. One freed terrorist in exchange for clean water. Too bad for the preacher. He won't be needed after all."

And with that last statement, the patient passed out.

CHAPTER TWELVE

"Shit!" Agony looked at Pain. "Doro doesn't have much time."

"Then let's not waste any more of it here. But we'll need to take him with us. I have a few more questions I need answers to." He turned to Ignatius. "Patch him up, Doc. We need to take him on a road trip."

"What the fuck?" She rushed to the corner and snatched a cell phone out of Iggy's hands. She was more pissed off at herself than she was with the so-called mortician. He had done what he'd been paid to do, which was to keep his employers informed. She was the professional who should have known enough to keep an eye on him.

After a quick scroll through the most recent texts, she recognized a number from the phone she'd copied from Tonio at Zaza's.

Her gaze flashed to Pain. "We'll have company soon."

"Anyone we know?"

"The Camorra. They know where we are and who we are."

"Who we are? Zaza knows you but I was never formally introduced."

"True." She read the text. "But if I am the Butch Bitch, you must be the psycho commando." Her brow creased in a frown as she shook her head. "It makes no sense, though. We're here looking for Doro. Why the hell would the Camorra come to stop us? They have nothing to do with the terrorists."

"That we know of. Now that I think about it, though, it makes perfect sense."

He seemed to hesitate as he looked at the now passed-out terrorist.

"You'll have to explain it later. We need to go," she reminded him, "and we need to go now!"

"Patch him up, Doc, enough that he can survive a short journey."

Ignatius was terrified but shook his head. "He has lost considerable blood and that bullet is next to the femoral artery. One wrong move and he'll bleed out before you know what's going on."

"What's going on is that you were so busy texting that you missed my surgical display." Pain threw the bullet he had extracted at his head. "A few quick stitches, which you can do faster than I can, and we can remove the tourniquet and get the fuck out of here."

Iggy's frustration—he did, after all, once take the Hippocratic Oath—warred with his fears. "Even with stitches, if you move him without a stretcher and an ambulance, he may still very well die on you before you leave the parking lot. If you want him dead, fine, but I won't have you come back and blame me because your corpse isn't able to answer any of your questions."

"Listen, you—"

"Cars!" Agony shouted.

Pain shut up long enough to hear several engines roar to screeching stops. He wanted to break something, specifically Ignatius's neck.

"We'll find something else," she pleaded. "But right now, we are out of time."

They had left the front door open when they'd entered and could hear car doors being opened but not closed, rounds being chambered, and several hushed voices. The angle of the small vestibule at the front gave them some cover as Gus' gang came through the front door and they rushed out the back as quickly and quietly as possible.

Three armed men were about to open the back door when it flew open. Pain eliminated the first two with a punch to the neck of one and a crotch kick to the other. Agony settled for a good old-fashioned roundhouse kick to the head of the third and she gathered the guns as quickly as she could as they hurried around the side of the building toward the parking lot.

Most of the gang was inside and busy searching rooms and interrogating Ignatius. Only two were left out front but seemed to have no training in how to properly keep an eye out during a developing situation. They were both unconscious and kissing gravel before they had a chance to notice that they'd left a blind spot.

The partners reached their Buick, although she still wasn't sure they had any legal status to claim it as theirs. Whoever the car belonged to, it now had four slashed tires. They split up and scurried through the dozen parked cars, looking for keys left in the ignitions. He took the right side and she took the left and they met and hunched down in the middle.

"I have a Cadillac Escalade," he said, "and a Subaru hatchback whose back half is filled with speakers, the better to annoy you with when stopped next to it at a traffic light."

"I have a Mustang and a 'Vette," she announced. "Style points for my side, practicality points for yours. Besides, I've never ridden in a Caddie before."

"The Caddie it is." He flipped the key ring around on his finger. "It's big enough to fit half the Camorra mob and be visible from the moon."

They remained low, headed to the Caddie, and flung the other keys into the distance along the way—four fewer vehicles for anyone to follow them in. When they reached the rear of the Caddie, Agony held her hand out for the keys.

"What?" He didn't want to give them up. "Finders-drivers, losers-riders."

She snatched the keys and almost took his finger with them. "This is no time to stick to surface streets, Sir I Don't Like Freeways."

The doors were open and he took the shotgun seat grudgingly. No alarms went off but the interior light was noticeable enough in the early dawn darkness to give them away and several shots rang out as the Camorra emerged from the front of the mortuary.

"Give me a gun," Pain commanded.

"What? This is no time—"

"Give me a fucking gun!"

She handed him one that she had picked up from the goons out back and he slid out of the vehicle. He fired several shots back in the general vicinity of the front of the building, which made everyone who had emerged duck into cover and gave him enough time to play a hunch. He took a step back and took a shot at the rear passenger-side window.

The window ended up with nothing more than a small spider-web crack and he hopped inside.

"Bulletproof glass?" She started the engine.

"If any of their rides were going to have it, this would be the one."

She put the Caddie in gear and turned to face him because she had a very important question to ask. "Which way is north?"

"It's dawn on the east coast." He thought the answer was obvious. "Keep the rising sun on your right."

She pulled out and turned left. He looked out his window and saw the sun making its way lazily to the horizon with a touch of an orange glow. If they were at the beach, it would be a beautiful sunrise. Sadly, a day at the beach was not listed in their itinerary.

When they looked in the mirrors, they saw six cars accelerate out of the parking lot behind them and catch up rapidly.

"Don't floor it." Pain could almost hear Agony's thoughts as she ran through her choices of evasive maneuvers. She had once been a cop, one of the best, and he felt certain that she knew how to handle herself when she was behind the wheel. They needed to have a quick confab and that would be easier to do if they weren't squealing willy-nilly through the streets.

"Give me one good reason why I shouldn't work the pedal on the right to its maximum potential?"

"Partner to partner," he asked, "what do we know about our current situation?"

"We have an ass-load of Camorra's on our asses." It was hard but she kept her right foot steady and applied only moderate pressure.

"And our asses are protected inside a vehicle with bulletproof glass."

She nodded her agreement. "We are headed to an unknown destination." She decided to play along with the partner game.

"How much gas did they leave us with?"

She checked the gauge "A quarter of a tank."

"And in this behemoth, that gives us what? Thirty miles before we end up driving on fumes?"

"About that." She sighed. "I guess that takes the outrunning them on the freeway option off the table."

"And I assume that even if we had a full tank and hit a freeway, the preacher—Doro," he corrected himself. He admired her desire to remember the name of a victim. "Doro would be dead by the time we lost anyone on our tail and had to turn back to try to determine our unknown destination."

"Slow and steady wins the race." She smiled. Although she had always envisioned herself as the hare, it never won. In the race to save Doro, she wanted to come out as the winner.

"This time, streets are our best friends." He tossed out another thought. "If they have us outnumbered and on a freeway, they might manage to block us in and produce an accident that would leave an immediate ten-mile back-up of fender-benders in its wake. No amount of glass is bulletproof enough to withstand a barrage of bullets—that the Camorra gang no doubt has—for the hour that it would take for any first-responders to reach the front of the commotion."

"If we stay on the city streets, they could produce a fender-bender at any stoplight," she pointed out.

"Yes," he agreed, "they could. But this is one of their vehicles— probably one of their main ones so they know about the bullet-proof windows. They could ram us from behind on a corner in front of a Starbucks, but that doesn't mean we have to step out and exchange insurance information. I'm very sure that since they don't want to draw any more attention from your former friends in blue than we do, all they will do is tag-team and keep us under surveillance."

"Which brings me back to my earlier point. It makes no sense that the Camorra have invited themselves to the party."

Pain shrugged. "The way I see it, there are two options. The first is that they put the word out to all their contacts for information on us but honestly, that's weak. I can't see Iggy calling them before he alerted the big, bad terrorists."

She nodded and waited impatiently for him to continue.

"The second is far more likely." He tapped his fingers on the dashboard and she tried to ignore it. "The terrorists don't want visibility at this point so it works for them to enlist someone to deal with us. They have a wide network and a huge budget and would know what happened at the Noir. Zaza and his gang are the perfect choice for someone to do the grunt work. We humiliated them very publically—inadvertently, of course, but the result is still the same—and they will want retribution and to rebuild their rep. That aside, they have a hit on you they want to collect on. If they get paid a little extra to do the same job, that's the kind of money they won't refuse."

"Okay…" She wasn't completely convinced. "So Iggy was told to call them if he had a problem. I can buy that but why follow us when killing us is what they ultimately want? We'd have no chance in a concerted attack."

"My guess is that their instructions were to keep us occupied if they didn't kill us outright. That way, they will still be able to fulfill their objective once they've given the terrorists the time they need to deal with Doro."

"And once he's gone—shit!" She wanted to throw the Caddie in reverse and start her own fender-bender pile-up as she went from car to car and placed strategic shots into any forehead she could find. Unfortunately, she knew they would be seriously outnumbered and they and Doro would probably end up on the other side of life as they knew it.

"Slow and steady wins the race," he reminded her. "We can't outrun or lose them all so make it look like you're driving in an effort to shake them. If you succeed, great. If you don't, it will at least give us time to try to decide where our destination might be."

Agony made a few quick turns without signaling her intentions in advance by turning on a blinker.

No shots rang out from behind them. Maybe Pain had been right about the Caddie's invincibility. She drove on through the familiar city streets.

"Dog walker," her partner pointed out when he was the first to see someone about to cross the street ahead of them leading two small dogs and, heaven have mercy, a Great Dane to a small green space to do their business.

She braked. "How many kinds of wrong career paths does someone have to make," she wondered acerbically, "to end up on the street at sunrise with plastic bags in their pockets for the singular purpose of picking dog shit up?"

"I don't know." He watched them cross. "But I have more respect for the walker than I do for the owners of a Great Dane who think apartment living is the ideal space for such a magnificent animal."

Their back bumper hadn't been bumped yet, but the Camorra lead car was still directly behind them and she had to admit that her partner had nailed their strategy. She drove to the next corner and turned right, then cursed when they were suddenly stuck behind a school bus.

A dozen or so kids took their sweet time to climb up the stairs and disappear while proud parents watched their Mensa-bound progenies head off to another day of hair pulling and fart jokes.

"Try one more turn," Pain suggested as the bus pulled away.

"Right or left?"

"Half a block ahead. Make a U and use the sidewalk to come back and pick me up."

She didn't even have time to ask what he intended before he slid out. As instructed, she drove half a block before she made a very illegal U-turn in the middle of the street.

With horns blaring in her wake, she noticed a large group of early morning cyclists and their bikes sprawled in the middle of the street to block all traffic in both directions. Her partner stood on the other side of the carnage and waited patiently for his ride.

As instructed, she took the sidewalk and it seemed no one was willing to argue with an Escalade. Once she'd passed the mayhem, she veered onto the street and slowed enough for him to be able to open the door and jump in.

"Now," he advised, "would be a perfect time to apply pressure on the pedal on the right and do some of those evasive maneuvers you cop people are so familiar with."

Agony took the advice and a minute later, they were in the clear.

"I've always wanted to do that," Pain said cheerfully.

"Do what?" She was beginning to believe the man might be certifiably insane.

"Bust up a group of cyclists during rush hour traffic who block an entire lane because they want to get their morning ride in. Are the bicycles registered? No! Do they have to pay for license plates? No! If they did, some of the money from the registration and plates could go to help maintain the roads they seem to think they have every right to."

She burst out laughing. The man had a pet peeve after all. He must be at least half-human.

"How do you feel about joggers?" she asked.

"They always run against traffic so they know enough to be able to step out of the way. I have no gripes with the runners."

Now that they had lost their tails, she pulled to the side of the road and requested that they swap seats. He obliged without bothering to ask why.

Once this was accomplished and he put the Caddie in gear, she explained.

"We need to find Doro and I think better when my hands are busy."

Pain expected her to reach into her bloodstained coat and pull out one of the many guns she had confiscated in the last twenty-four hours and start cleaning it. What he saw instead was a ball of yarn and two knitting needles. She seemed to be working on a scarf now judging by the click-clack of her needles as they added straight rows one way, then the other.

He drove slowly and circled blocks, fearful of heading too far in the wrong direction since neither of them had yet thought of a viable destination.

"What did the man with a bullet in his leg say at the end?" she asked between a needle-click here and a needle-clack there. He had to fight back an urge to start humming "Old McDonald Had

A Farm." *With a click-clack here and a click-clack there. Here a click, there a clack, everywhere a click-clack.*

"He said all kinds of things—half of it probably bullshit."

"What did he say about where the preacher was being held?"

Pain searched his memory. "Something about moldy bread and rats."

"Yeah." She paused in her knitting. "That stuck with me too. I have a best guess."

She put the needles and yarn away and he wondered how many pockets were on the inside of her long coat.

"He's being held at Flipple's," she said in all seriousness.

"What the fuck is a Flipple?" he responded, equally serious.

"I can tell you weren't raised in these here parts. Pull over, cowboy. We're changing seats again."

He had made it a habit to never argue with a crazy woman and did as instructed. Once they had both buckled in again, he moved his gaze constantly from mirror to mirror as the crazy woman drove on and explained.

"Flipple's was a local cereal brand. Each box was filled with animal shapes but here was the kicker. The little animals never got soft and soggy. As a kid, you would scoop the animals out of the milk that had been poured onto them, tip your spoon to let the milk drain out, and flip whatever animal you'd managed to corner on your spoon into the air and try to catch it in your mouth on its way down. When all the animals had been caught and flipped, you would tip the bowl and drink the milk."

"It must have made for some very messy breakfast tables." Still, he liked the thought of the hand-eye coordination that had to be executed to successfully finish a bowl.

"Oh yeah," Agony agreed. "Messy was the name of the game."

"I assume it never caught on nationally?"

"Sadly, no."

Pain gave her time to mourn her childhood memory.

"They closed the factory a decade ago when Mr. Flipple

suddenly died of a heart attack and no one was able to take up the leadership." She resumed the story with only a faint trace of regret in her tone. "The land the factory was built on was not worth selling. It was easier to simply leave the building and all its stored grains to rot."

"An abandoned factory with moldy grains and rats." He couldn't have come up with a better scenario for the terrorists' purposes.

"This will be a touchy subject," he said as she drove confidently toward the warehouse district and the abandoned factory, "but do you have any friends in the department? I mean at least one who you could still trust with your life."

"You are correct, that's a very touchy subject. Why do you ask?"

"The wounded man said the city was willing to strike a deal. We need to try to stop it before they complete the trade-off with the terrorists for the water plant. Doro's isn't the only life at stake here."

Since both of them were wanted by one agency or another, they were understandably reluctant to involve the authorities, but it was a chance they had to take.

She took advantage of the Caddie's built-in phone system, pressed speaker, and dialed a number.

CHAPTER THIRTEEN

It was early enough for the night and the day shifts to have recently exchanged greetings and farewells but late enough for the daily assignments and roll-out to have been completed.

After several rings, Agony's call was answered.

"Fifth Precinct." The curt greeting irritated her. No "how may I direct your call?" No "if this is an emergency, please hang up and call nine-one-one." The woman's voice sounded like it was as crisp this early in the day as it would be when her shift ended eight hours later, which essentially meant that she was already bored to tears.

"I need the bullpen, please." She tried to sound firm but gentle, "I am trying to reach Sergeant Jeffries."

"Personal or business?"

"Business."

"Name?"

"Herman Melville." Pain gave her an odd look that seemed to also be infused in the voice on the other end of the phone.

"Funny," the woman responded, "You don't sound like a Herman."

"I am placing a call for Herman Melville," she explained with exaggerated patience. "He is the one who needs to speak to Sergeant Ishmael Jeffries."

"Business or personal?" It seemed the confusion over the name had thrown the woman off and she needed to rewind a few beats.

"Business," Agony repeated and restrained a sigh.

"Transferring now."

"Bullpen." A man answered after several rings.

"I'm calling for Jeffries," she said briskly. "Is the sergeant in?"

"Who shall I say is calling?"

"Captain Ahab."

"Hey, Sarge!" the man called. "I got one of your Dicksters on line two."

The line went silent as Agony was put on hold.

"Call me Ishmael," a seasoned voice said briskly. "Am I speaking to Moby or one of the minnows?"

"A minnow." She was pleased to hear her old sergeant's voice again. "Definitely a minnow at this point."

After a short pause, the sergeant responded with, "Nine minus one."

She hung up and explained briefly to Pain that even though every call through the phone system was recorded, a cop who was knowledgeable about telephone wiring had found a spare line in a phone closet years earlier. He had connected that number directly to an old single-line relic of a phone that sat in cubicle number nine.

"Cube Nine," she finished as she counted down what she thought was one minute, "is not assigned to anyone. It's where paperwork goes to die. The phone there is only used when a cop has a CI calling. No call in Cube Nine can be recorded or traced. That phone is the closest thing to sacred as you can find in the entire station."

When one minute had passed, she dialed quickly.

"They can take the Agony out of the force." Her old sergeant answered on the first ring. "But they can't take the force out of the Agony. Don't dawdle."

Dawdling was the last thing she could afford to do. She and the sarge could catch up on chit-chat another time. With a glance at Pain, she gave her report in the concise manner Jeffries preferred.

"The city is working on a deal with a small terrorist cell to release a prisoner. The only name I have is Budria. I can't confirm if that is the prisoner's name or not but the city can't go through with it. Some small bad things might happen if they don't do the deal, but some extremely big bad things will happen if they do."

"And you know this how?"

"It doesn't matter how, Sarge. All that matters is that I know it."

She knew Jeffries wouldn't doubt the veracity of her report but he would have to face some serious risks to his reputation and ass when he attempted to pass the message up the food chain.

"A terrorist cell and Budria? That's all you're giving me to go on?"

Pain pantomimed drinking a glass of water.

"And a threat on a water treatment plant. If that's not enough info to get someone's attention, that will prove that they don't want this out in the open. A lot of lives are in danger."

"How many lives?" He needed to know how hard to push. "Dozens?"

"Higher."

"Hundreds?"

"Higher."

That was not the answer that a simple sergeant in the force wanted to have as his responsibility.

He took a moment to reduce the number to one.

"You know, kid, you are a person of interest in some serious shit that's gone down in the last few days. It might be wise to turn yourself in so everyone can sort that all out."

"I wish I could but I have a slight trust issue with everyone at the moment. Aside from that, there is something I have to do first."

"You can't save everyone, kid." Even Pain could hear the touch of sadness in the gruff voice. "But I couldn't get that through to you in training so I somehow doubt that you'll listen to me now."

"Do you remember what I said as a rookie?" Agony smiled at the memory of her younger self and the weathered veteran.

"Yeah." Jeffries chuckled. "I remember a tall skinny white girl who seemed to be nothing more than knees and elbows looking me right in the eyes and saying, 'I can try, Sarge. I can try.'"

"My attitude hasn't changed since then, Sarge. I hope yours hasn't either. I've seen you use that hard head of yours to bust through bureaucratic walls before. I hope it hasn't gotten soft in your old age because these are some serious walls that need to be knocked down."

"I'll see what I can do but you better stock up on Excedrin. I suspect you'll end up feeding them to me through a straw to relieve the headache I will come out of this with."

"I'll arrange for an IV drip if you come through for me."

There was a pause before he asked his last question.

"More than hundreds, you said?"

"Many more."

"Shit."

The line went dead.

"So…" Pain offered his assessment of how the call went. "You did leave at least one unburned bridge in your wake."

"Some bridges are built of sterner stuff than others." She continued to wind through the streets to the factory. "Sarge has every right to be cynical. After decades on the force, he has seen it all. When I think about it, he is the only one I've ever met who has turned promotions down."

"That makes him a strange breed indeed." His respect for the man went up several notches.

"He once told me he didn't know if his given name was a blessing or a curse." Pain listened as she drove. He could see her trying to catch a memory.

"It was during a quiet moment when I dropped by his desk to ask him a question about an assignment I'd been given. He listened to my concerns, then told me that Ishmael was the name of the Patriarch Abraham's firstborn son, whose birthright was taken from him under dubious circumstances. It was also the name of the narrator of the novel *Moby Dick*. He said he chose to focus on the novel rather than the scriptures as he tried to prepare us for what we had to do each day."

Damn, Pain thought. *I'd love to spend a night in front of a warm fire with this guy.*

"'There is no great white whale!' That's how he would greet us before he handed out our daily assignments. 'This city is nothing but a small pond where the big fish try to eat the little fish. Don't let the big fish win, little minnows. You have them outnumbered and as long as you all stick together, justice can be served. Now, go nibble away.'"

"Huh," he eventually said after he'd taken that in. "There ought to be a group called Nibblers Anonymous. I would raise my hand at every meeting and say, 'Hi, I'm M and I'm a Nibbler.'"

Agony was glad she hadn't taken a sip of coffee at that moment because she would have snorted it out through her nose. She took one hand off the wheel and raised it as she confessed to the imaginary meeting, "Hi. I'm A and I'm a Nibbler."

"I am," he continued as an attendee in the imaginary meeting, "paranoid, prone to violence, and almost unfit for interactions between civilized humans."

She remained silent as he continued to share.

"But I served my country and nibbled away. Some nibbles were more successful than others, but a large number of bad people are now no longer among the living and a larger number of innocent people are still alive to watch their grandchildren grow up. I am a Nibbler and proud of it."

Agony took up where he left off.

"I was part of the force in blue. I did my best. And although the city I was born and raised in and swore to protect and serve might never remember my name, the innocents I helped will live long enough to enable them to kiss their grandchildren." She smiled apologetically at him for having stolen that line.

"I guess there is no honor amongst thieves after all," he responded amidst laughter.

"And," she continued, "although I no longer wear the blue or the badge, I vow to continue to be a Nibbler."

"Time!" He brought the meeting to an end. "It's time for the pledge. I am a Nibbler."

"I am a Nibbler," she repeated.

"I will stay anonymous to the best of my abilities." He made it up the best he could.

She repeated the second line of the pledge before she helped him by adding the third line. "And I vow to never stop nibbling. Fuck the big fish!"

"Fuck the big fish!" he repeated before he added, "And may God smile upon the nibblers."

"There it is." Her statement confirmed that their Nibblers Anonymous meeting had officially drawn to its conclusion. She had put the Caddie in park in front of a huge facility that he could only assume was the former Flipples' factory.

"Can we circle the block?" he asked.

"A block is square." She could hold her own with his semantics. "How do you circle a square?"

"Drive to the end of the street," he replied calmly but admired her snark. "Take a left, then a left, and another left so we end up where we began."

"Well, hell, why didn't you say so?"

Agony drove the Caddie slowly like a real estate investor surveying the abandoned plant that took up the whole block and they both studied the property in silence.

"There are no vehicles except on the southeast corner," he observed once they returned to their original position.

"I saw the same."

They were about to debate their best options for how to rescue Doro when a phone rang somewhere in one of her coat pockets. She dug her cell out and when she saw that the call came from Cubicle Nine, she put it on speaker and trusted Pain to keep his silence.

"If you love me," she answered, "please hang up now. If you hate me, please hold. As soon as I am done with my current round of being spanked, you will be the next in line. This call is not being recorded but is being put on speaker. There is a gentleman here who lives to hear me being humiliated."

"Does that gentleman have a name?" Sergeant Jeffries asked.

"The name is Pain," he said in response. "Manifest Pain."

"You motherfucker," the man shouted as loudly as he could while in Cube Nine. "If you harm one hair on her head—"

"He's a good guy, Sarge." Agony interrupted the introductions and frowned at the psycho who had now gone from using Macarena to Manifest as his first name. *How long will it take him before he pulls Margarita out?*

"He's also a major pain in the ass." She hurried the conversation along. "But we are in this together."

"You two sound like a match made in heaven," the sergeant told her, "which helps to confirm my belief that there is a God and that He has one hell of a sense of humor."

"Hey, Sarge." Pain thought it was as good a time as any to join the conversation. "You piss on her, you piss on me."

"Then that will save me a shit-load of trouble," Jeffries retorted, "because I have just been pissed on from great heights for having even mentioned a terrorist threat, a water plant, and a prisoner release in the same sentence. I had to bust my hard-headed skull through more than a handful of bureaucratic walls to even get to a place where I could have the dubious honor of the conversation."

"Sorry, Sarge," Agony interjected. "I shouldn't have dragged you into it."

"Too late." He brushed her apology aside. "I also had to dodge a snow-balling pile of shit that rolled down the hill from the same heights for having suggested how they should handle the situation. It didn't help my case when they claimed there was no one named Budria, Buddha, or Bootylicious listed as a prisoner anywhere."

"It's okay, Sarge." She tried to cut his rampage off before he raised his voice loud enough to draw attention to Cube Nine.

"Nothing about this is okay," he insisted and made a hissing sound to reinforce it. She had never heard him hiss before. "Someone somewhere is doing something they don't want the press to know about—or anyone else for that matter. The water you are now taking a dip in contains a significant number of sharks."

"But us minnows have the sharks outnumbered." She tried to sound confident.

"The math may be on the minnows' side," her former sergeant replied, "but there is a Moby out there and I'm fresh out of Captain Ahabs. The harpoons will be aimed at me soon when they begin to wonder how I know what I think I know and who I heard it from."

"Then tell the harpoon-holding Internal Affairs officer nothing but the truth." It was the first time she had ever given him advice. She did not expect him to laugh at it but laugh he did.

"Yeah, me playing nice with the Rat Squad. Dream on. I can take care of my ass with them in here. You be careful with your pain-in-the-ass self out there and try to live long enough to fill me in before I decide to hang it all up and join Merk and his friend in Belize."

"Will do, Sarge," she managed to add before the line went dead.

"No Budria?" Agony turned to Pain as they surveyed the huge abandoned factory. "Could that mean that maybe the terrorists' schemes have already been thwarted?"

"I doubt it." He shook his head. "The name never sounded right to me. It sounded more like a code name and it also sounded familiar, but fuck my brain if I can remember why."

"All right." She tried to draw their focus back to their current situation, which was seated outside a huge complex they had to find a way to infiltrate. "Fuck Budria." She made her decision after a moment's thought. "The city either will or won't make a deal. Somewhere in there is an innocent minister and I'm going in for him."

"Roll forward quietly." He nodded, focused on the matter at hand. "And try to find an innocuous parking space. We are about to stay righteous."

She looked solemnly at him for a long moment. "That's the third time I've heard you use the phrase 'stay righteous.' It was one of Chaz's, wasn't it?"

"Yeah." He smiled sadly at her. "So was 'never eat the yellow snow' but at least he had the grace to acknowledge that he'd pilfered it from Zappa. I never knew who he stole 'stay righteous' from but he lived it every day and that's all anyone can ask for from a mortal."

Agony eased closer to the southeast corner where a handful of vehicles were parked. She chose her parking place and they climbed out. They weren't looking at Captain Ahab's or Jonah's whale, or even Pinocchio's for that matter, but the building was a behemoth and they were about to enter its belly and try to give it a serious case of indigestion.

CHAPTER FOURTEEN

As they closed the Caddie's doors quietly, Agony searched through her coat's pockets and pulled out the smallest gun she could find amongst the many she had confiscated that day. It was a snub-nosed eight-shot revolver and she tried to give it to Pain.

"Nah, I'm fine." He shook his head. "I appreciate the offer but if I need a gun, I'm sure I can find someone inside who will be willing to leave me theirs in their will."

"Oh, come on!" His insane reluctance to use firearms had begun to seriously annoy her. "It only weighs twelve ounces so it's not like it'll weigh you down."

"And you have at least six more in the pockets of your magical mystery coat. That has to add at least eight pounds to your total weight."

"Oh, great." She shoved the weapon into one of her pockets again. "So now you're saying I'm fat?"

"I'm only saying that your coat gives you more bounce to the ounce than any coat should rightfully give."

"I plan to be buried in this coat," she informed him.

"And I plan to hire eight pallbearers instead of six to carry you, your coat, and your coffin out to the hearse. A funeral is no time for anyone to have to suffer from a hernia."

They were at a stand-off and they hadn't even entered the lion's den yet.

Pain straightened to his full height and held his arms at his sides. "I've seen you in action over the last few days. I know you can take my head off with a roundhouse kick. Please try to do it now."

"Are you fucking serious?"

"Dead serious." If he had to piss her off to make his point, he was willing to face any future fallout. "I'll bet you Doro's life that you will fail and both end up dead if you can't deliver the kick."

Agony used both hands to give her coat a quick flip to keep it out of her leg's way and a split second later, she sprawled on her back and stared at the sky. All he had done was give her a palm-shove to her chest.

"There's too much weight in the coat." He blocked the moon out as he stood over her. "You have your gun and your fantabulous baton. That's all you need. Any extra weight in your coat will slow you. Besides, those extra guns must have some bad karma because none of their former owners now have them in their possession."

He offered her a hand up and she took it as a way to acknowledge that he had a point.

Once on her feet, she searched her pockets and placed every confiscated weapon carefully in a neat pile next to the Caddie in case they were needed for future use.

"Mission objective?" he asked once she was eight pounds lighter.

"The pastor." She drew a deep breath as she studied the factory again. "The preacher, the minister...my Doro is in there somewhere. This mission's objective is extraction."

"Best guess, former best cop," Pain asked as he scanned the scene, "as to where he's being held?"

"Somewhere low." Agony recalled the former hostage for payment situations she'd been involved with while on the force. "If their plans go haywire again and they still need him alive, they'll want to be able to reach their escape vehicles as quickly as possible."

He couldn't argue with that assessment and considered the best plan of attack.

"No visible lights are on in any of the office windows, so he is being held in an internal room. There is only a handful of cars, so I'm guessing what…maybe a dozen guards max?"

"Maybe a baker's dozen plus three."

"I've always preferred having the higher ground."

"So what will you do? Scale the highest grain silo and come down from above like a thunderbolt from Zeus?"

Although he liked the image, he went with a more practical approach.

"We go in together and try to stay quieter than the rats that have called this place home for the last several decades while we do a little reconnaissance—stealth over gunfire. Everyone is guarding only one room. If we locate it, we have located Doro. The preacher is yours. Everyone else is mine but I go first. Oh, and I always take the hallway to the left."

Pain didn't give her time to argue as he strode to the short set of external stairs that led to a small deck in front of the only door in sight. He opened the door calmly and entered. A moment later, two bodies were tossed out through the door and landed on the deck. He emerged, threw them off and onto the ground, and gave her a thumbs-up as he disappeared inside again.

Agony took that as a sign that initial access had now been assured and rushed forward, up the stairs, and through the door. She stopped in a hallway that led both to the left and the right.

Her partner was nowhere in sight but she recalled his odd statement of his preferred direction and turned right. His admonition for stealth uppermost, she left her trusty S & W in her pocket as she flipped her baton open in her right hand. Her left hand and both feet were readily available should an occasion call for them.

As she followed the hallway, she realized that the rooms to her left were nothing more than offices. She turned and walked backward as she knocked on each door, opened it, did not enter to inspect it, and called, "No one in here," before she moved on, always walking backward.

After she'd knocked on the third door and stepped past it, a man emerged from the office with his gun drawn, ready to shoot her in the back. Before he could act, she snapped her baton on his wrist, broke it, and slapped the back of his head.

She didn't care if the second baton blow had killed him or simply left him unconscious. Her only focus was to clear the floor one room at a time.

Down the hallway that led left, Pain wasn't quite as subtle. Not knowing how solid any of the doors would be after two decades of rotting, he simply directed a kick at each doorknob and let whatever was left of it do most of the damage to whoever was hiding behind it.

The first two doors exposed nothing but old and moldy offices. The third, however, made him almost work up a sweat as splinters sprayed in all directions, as did his fists and feet when kicking the door in met with some resistance.

"Sorry about that," he said cheerfully when he saw a splinter lodged in a man's neck. "I could offer you advice but previous experience has taught me that you won't take it."

He moved to the next door without waiting for him to pull out the splinter and bleed out.

Two rooms later, the door opened before he had a chance to kick it in and he faced a man who held a two-barreled shotgun aimed directly at his chest.

"You loaded the wrong barrel," he pointed out casually.

The man looked at the weapon and was about to inform him

that he had both barrels loaded when the gun was snatched out of his hands. The stock was swung first into his balls and then on the back of his bowed head.

"You might live," Pain informed the man who was now bleeding on the musty-smelling tiled floor. "Then again, you might not but that is not my decision to make."

On Agony's side, her knock on the sixth door was met with a rapid-fire bullet barrage.

"Ohhh!" she cried in her best death-scream voice. *You can't blame me for the lack of stealth on this one, Pain. He's the one who fired!*

The shooter rushed out to see who he'd killed but didn't have the pleasure of learning her name. She swung her baton into the back of his neck and he sprawled at her feet. Had he been a Camorra his last thoughts might have been of the glory he would have earned for having taken the Butch Bitch down.

She ventured to the end of the hallway and wondered how the psycho commando was doing.

The thought was answered when moments later, they both opened the doors to their respective hallways at the same time, made eye contact, and nodded approval of their respective survival.

The scene in front of them was what had once been a factory floor. A convoluted series of conveyor belts had once held boxes waiting to be filled with Flipples funneled from above. Long-gone workers had done the best they could to make sure every box had at least one plastic-wrapped Flipple animal card dropped into it.

Collect all twelve Flipple animals. She remembered the campaign. *Cash them in for a free box so you can start your collection again.* She had acquired three free boxes that way. Given her devotion to the cereal, her mother had told her that the company would never go out of business if she continued to eat them with such dedication. When it did go out of business, not only did she have to go through Flipples withdrawal but she also had to deal with the guilt of knowing that if she had continued her quest to eat enough to get a fourth free box, she might have helped their finances enough for them to have remained profitable.

Of course, that was a long, un-moldy factory floor ago. From their respective positions, they could both see a small raised office in the middle of the space where the shift foremen and associates had no doubt once watched over the production lines.

Pain pointed at Agony, then at the raised office. He held two guns up that he had taken from those who no longer needed them. His message was clear. Her goal was the office. His was to cover her back. She began to think that she might end up not hating him after all.

"Olly olly oxen free motherfuckers!" he shouted as he strode onto what was left of the factory floor. She decided to make it a personal mission of hers to teach him a better line.

Several shots rang out from behind the machinery, all aimed at the big man. He fired at the equipment and forced the assailants to either jump or run. She dropped five more terrorists before the shooting stopped.

On the other hand, she thought, *if it ain't broke, don't fix it.*

After the echoes of gunfire faded, they approached the raised office from their respective angles and no other shots were fired. Either they had killed or run off any of the would-be terrorists or their enemies had run out of ammo.

The door to the office opened and two people emerged. The first was a short, thin, African with a gun held to his head by a much taller Anglo. Neither partner doubted that Doro was still alive.

One of his pant legs had been cut off and there was a bandage on his thigh, probably Ignatius' handiwork. A strip of gauze was wrapped around the top of his head as well. Iggy had done his best to keep the preacher alive until he was no longer needed.

"One trigger pull," the Anglo shouted, "and the preacher is dead!"

Agony made eye contact with Pain and shook her head. He wasn't happy about it but it was her gig and he would back his partner's play, whatever the fuck it was. Still, he hoped it didn't lead to her or him on one of Iggy's slabs.

"Listen to me, man with the gun." She forced the man she didn't think was a die-hard terrorist, anarchist, or radical to focus on her. "The big man over there and I have just eliminated all your backups."

"How do I know that?" he retorted.

"Because we are both here," she answered as calmly as she could, "and they are not."

Pain had to give her points for being able to point out obvious truths.

"And we will both put our guns down if you will trade the preacher for me."

And she thinks I'm the one who is insane? He held his guns up, then placed them on the floor. Their only purpose had been for him to shoot at the machinery as a distraction and he had no desire to use one now to bring death from a distance, no matter how tempting it was.

"I trade you for the preacher?"

"Me." She held the keys to the Caddie up. "And the keys to an escape vehicle."

The man didn't know if he could trust her or not but at this point, all he wanted to do was to get the fuck out of a bad situation he wasn't being paid enough to be in.

She held her arms out and walked backward toward the man who held the preacher with a gun to his head.

"I let the preacher go and I walk out of here with you and the keys?"

"That is the deal." She held the keys out behind her.

When he tried to snatch them from her, she held on firmly. "You let go of the preacher and I'll let go of the keys."

Finally, the man released Doro, grabbed the keys and Agony from behind, and held his gun at her head as he walked her toward the door. He felt safe as he watched the preacher stumble to the big man and they both stared at him, helpless to stop him.

"I think," the man said to Pain, "that neither of you is worth leaving as witnesses."

He moved the gun from her head for a second to take his two shots. She used that split second to jab behind her with a knitting needle and made direct contact as she rammed it through one of his eyes and spun to fell him with a neck punch.

Agony pulled the needle out of the man's eye and looked at Pain with a smile.

"Knit one, pearl two. Are we done here now?"

Doro was wobbly and weak but able to walk slowly with a little assistance. She rushed to him and the pastor was profuse in giving his thanks to God and his two rescuers.

"My name is Alicia Goni." She rushed the introduction. "We will take you to your congregation now."

"What is his name?" Doro asked and nodded at Pain.

"He hasn't told me yet but it begins with an M."

"Ahh." The pastor nodded. "Like Michael, the fighting archangel."

"Michael Pain, yes." He looked at her. "See? That wasn't too hard, now was it?"

She shook her head. "We need to hurry."

Her partner scooped Doro into his arms and followed as she led the way to the door.

"You must get to the boat," the pastor insisted as they hurried through the building.

"What boat?" Pain asked while Agony made sure that no other guards were waiting in ambush.

"I don't know the name." Doro sounded apologetic for having

failed to learn it. "I only know they are planning to take a boat to escape once their comrade is released and bad things will soon follow."

"What kind of bad things?" He had to turn sideways as he carried the preacher down the hallway so he didn't bump either the man's bandaged head or leg against a wall.

"I don't know details but I heard about a bomb."

"Confirmation number two," he called to make sure that Agony had heard it. She nodded.

"I only hear this because they talk freely in front of a man they will soon kill. But there is a boat. You must find the boat."

"We'll have to split up." Pain set the man on his feet when they reached the door. "I'll look into the boat. You get the shepherd to his flock."

CHAPTER FIFTEEN

Agony slid one of Doro's arms around her shoulder and opened the door. Half a dozen cars raced down the road that led to the parking lot.

"I am sorry," the preacher said. "At least you tried. That is all God can ask."

"Shit!" her partner cursed and kicked himself mentally. "They didn't have to keep tailing us. The fucking Caddie probably has a GPS."

He slammed the door and rushed down the hallway.

"For a good angel," Doro commented with a smile, "he swears like a devil."

Pain scooped up one of the guards who had not survived his earlier encounter with her and flung him over his shoulder as he hurried back.

"You hide with the real preacher until the coast is clear and then leave," he instructed. "I'll head to the Caddie with the fake preacher. Hopefully, they'll all go after me. I'll catch up with you later."

Again, he gave her no time to argue with his plan but flung

the door open, rushed down the steps, and jogged to the Caddie as the Camorra hit squad roared into the parking lot.

Agony and Doro took a step back into the shadows but peeked around the edge of the door enough to be able to watch the other man run with a dead "preacher" on his shoulders.

The six cars slid and screeched to a stop as shots rang out, aimed at the psycho commando and the hostage he was rescuing. Several of the shots would have been a direct hit if the dead body he carried hadn't stopped them.

He flung the corpse in the back of the Caddie and raced away. Agony was relieved when the other cars immediately followed.

"Be careful," she instructed the pastor, "but keep an eye out and shout if any other cars pull in."

"Where do you go?"

"I go to find keys." She rushed down the hallway. "Someone here must have been a driver."

Doro kept the door cracked open enough to peer out. She returned minutes later with four sets of keys in her hand, helped the man down the steps, and assisted him to walk to where the Caddie had been parked. Once she'd retrieved the stash of guns she had left there and distributed them in her coat pockets, they focused on the half-dozen cars left in the parking lot.

"I see a Jeep." He pointed at it. "It's not fast but very reliable."

She kept his arm around her shoulder as he limped toward the vehicle as quickly as he could while she sifted through the confiscated keys she held in her free hand. Fortunately, one of them was for their new ride. She helped the pastor into the passenger seat, climbed in behind the wheel, and accelerated away.

Even though she could see no tailing vehicles or other cars lying in wait, she still took several evasive maneuvers before she could relax. She was three minutes into their escape route when her phone rang. With a scowl, she fished it out of a pocket saw a number she didn't recognize.

It wasn't the number from the Caddie and the situation being what it was, she was in no mood for an automated sales pitch. Still, she felt the need to answer it because she realized that she and the psycho commando had never taken the time to exchange numbers in the hope of a second date call. He might have obtained hers somehow but she had failed to do the same. She told Doro to remain silent because if it wasn't her partner, she didn't want whoever was calling to know she had him.

Doro made the zip-the-lip motion and she put her cell on speaker.

"Hello?" she said cautiously.

"What do you know about the Spanish Civil War?" Pain asked.

"I'm guessing it was held in Spain," she quipped, "and there was probably nothing civil about it."

"Yay for you. You're two for two."

She could hear the ping of bullets ricocheting off the Caddie's bulletproof glass and hoped that the tires hadn't been shot out and he was now confined inside the vehicle in the midst of a shoot-out. The screech of tires making high-speed turns put an end to that concern.

At a loss, she looked at Doro to see if he had any idea what the other man was talking about. The pastor, recognizing the angel Michael's voice, wished he could add to the conversation but could only throw his hands up in the universally recognized sign of "I haven't got a clue."

"Francisco Ascaso Budria was an anarchist."

"Will you get to the point soon?" she shouted, "because otherwise, I don't care if he was an Anarchist or a Baptist or neo-physicist. The next time I see you, I shall shove some type of an ist right up your anal-ist cavity."

"He died in Barcelona during an assault on a shipyard."

"Many people die during assaults," she pointed out. "Our brief history together has proven that to be a very salient point."

"But he grunted, remember?"

"I wasn't in the ancient shipyard assault," she reminded him, "so I have no way to remember if the anarchist grunted or not."

"Not Budria himself, the anarchist with a bullet in his leg on Iggy's table. He said 'Captain,' grunted, then said 'Budria.'"

"I don't want to criticize your medical technique," she said although she was about to start critiquing his summarizing skills. "But I believe he grunted because you were dicking around with a bullet in his leg to keep him talking."

"What if he was about to say 'the captain of the Budria,' but his painful grunt got in the way of the 'of the?'"

"Then I would say," Agony answered dryly, "that you might have been a little heavy-handed with the scalpel."

"I'll try to do better next time." Another screech of tires and more window pings followed before he finally made his point. "We have Captain, grunt, and Budria, and a boat we are searching for but whose name we do not know."

"The Captain of the Budria? Do you think our mystery ship might be named the Budria?" To her, it sounded ridiculously plausible. "Spell Budria."

"B-u-d-r-i-a. The spelling is right but whether there is a boat called that is only a guess." Pain laughed and a sound of metal crunching suggested a couple of car bumpers being put to good use in the background.

"And how," she asked, "are we supposed to find out where this hypothetical ship is docked?"

"I don't know. Do you have any Ouija boards handy?"

"I know this one!" Doro shouted, thankful to finally be of use. "A member of the church, Bonyo, works for the Port Authority. Not at the shipyards but at the actual Port Authority. If I can call him, he can tell me yes or no if such a ship exists and where it is."

"Did you hear that?" she tried to shout over the commotion coming from the Caddie.

"Yeah!" Pain yelled in response. "Preacher, Bonyo, and Budria!"

"Roger that. We'll make the call."

"You do that, then pass me the mustard and I'll ketchup with you."

The rev of an engine and more screeching tires were followed by the sound of metal buckling.

"Caddie five!" her partner shouted. "Goon cars zero! I love this shit."

The call dropped.

"Some angels drive chariots," Doro informed her calmly. "It seems this particular one prefers Cadillacs."

Agony had to wonder if anyone had ever referred to Macarena Manifest Michael Pain as an angel before. She checked the gas gauge and discovered that they had at least commandeered a vehicle with a good supply of gas left in the tank before it would need to be filled.

She still saw no sign of a tail but remained alert and handed Doro her phone. The minister dialed and managed to put the device on speaker since that would be easier than trying to remember and pass the information along.

While it rang, she found a supermarket and pulled into a space on the outskirts of the parking lot—an old cop habit. Easy in and easy out. She then resorted to another old cop habit and retrieved a small notepad and pen from another of her magical long coat's inner pockets. *Write it down. Memory is not a trustworthy companion.*

"Port Authority." A Nigerian's lilting voice answered. "How may I help you?"

"Bonyo?" Doro asked.

"Pastor?"

"Shh, shh, shhh!" He tried to calm his parishioner. "Yes. Please stay quiet and listen. I need your help."

"Yes, yes." The man lowered his voice. "Tell me where you are. The prayer chains have continued non-stop and we will come and get you from your captivity."

"The prayers have already been answered, praise God," the pastor informed him, "and I am no longer captive. But I still need a little help, Brother Bonyo, and you are the only one who can provide it."

"Tell me where and how and I will be there as soon as possible."

From the tone in the man's voice, Agony could tell how beloved the short, thin, pastor was. It also confirmed the earnestness with which she had been hired to find him. Sometimes, her job as a PI sucked but she was so close to a happy ending on this one that any memories of less pleasant jobs immediately faded into the distant background.

"The where, Brother Bonyo," Doro instructed calmly but firmly, "is at your desk. The how is to see if you can find out any information on a ship that may be docked in the harbor."

"Is that where you are being held?"

"No, no. Please listen. I am no longer being held. But I need to know if there is a certain ship and if it exists, I need to know where it is. The name is Budria and I need to know it in all haste."

Phones rang in the background but they could also hear computer keys being punched frantically.

"It is not a cargo ship," Bonyo told them. "There is no cargo ship with that name docked in the harbor."

"Shit." The church-goers heard Agony curse but as far as cursing went, it was a mild one and at least wasn't blasphemous so they let it slide without any criticism.

She was both pissed and confused. With the threat of terror it held, she had expected a behemoth to be docked somewhere. Maybe Pain had it wrong and they were back to square one.

"Wait, wait." Bonyo continued to tap his keyboard. "I'm searching marinas now."

Wait and wait were two words that didn't sit well with her but fortunately, it only took one wait before he exclaimed, "I found her! She has a foreign registry and is a small pleasure cruiser.

Smaller than a yacht but big enough for the open seas as long as the weather is not too severe."

"Where is she?" Agony interjected before the conversation could shift direction to how big the boat was and how many passengers it could hold.

"She is currently docked in the Peasant's View Marina—and that seems strange."

"Strange in what way?" She tried to gather as much information as quickly as possible.

"The FA Budria is a pleasure cruiser," Bonyo explained. "The Peasant's View Marina is mostly for working fishermen's boats. It is not where I would expect it to be docked. It would be like parking a brand new Mercedes in a used car lot of old worker-vans."

"So…" She tried to get a visual in her mind, having not spent much of her life as either a commercial fisherman or as one of the beautiful people on a pleasure cruiser. "Once we get to the marina, it should be easy to locate?"

"It will be the only boat of its kind," the man assured her. "But if you have been invited to board, you should hurry. It is signed out to set off into international waters very soon."

She wrote the address down and punched it into the Jeep's GPS. While she knew the way to the pastor's community, from there to the dockside would be a whole different trip.

"Thank you, Bonyo!" She started the Jeep's engine. "I will take the pastor home now."

"Praise God, who hears our prayers!" Bonyo rejoiced. "Pastor, shall I call and let the people know?"

"No, Bonyo," Doro instructed and chuckled. "My safe return is a miracle and miracles are best received when they are not texted in advance."

Agony drove in the direction of the preacher's community. She wouldn't have a cab or an Uber driver finish her gig for her and calculated that she would have enough time to make her delivery and still reach the marina before the Budria hauled anchor or whatever the fuck boats did.

As they hurried through the streets, she held her hand out for her phone.

"You drive." Doro shook his head. "I dial."

"Hit redial minus one." She sighed, not appreciating the safe driving lesson no matter how well-intentioned.

Doro did as requested, put the phone on speaker, and held it out close enough to her ear so she could both hear and speak while keeping both eyes on the road and both hands on the wheel.

"I'm a little busy at the moment." Pain's voice held both urgency and mirth. "If anyone at home is keeping track of the score, it is now Caddie seven, goons still zero, but a hot dog cart vendor is not at all happy."

"The good ship FA Budria is docked in the Peasant's View Marina but is scheduled to hit the high seas soon."

"A marina? Not the harbor?"

Agony admired that he passed up a chance for self-congratulations at having guessed that the Budria was a boat.

"A marina, correct." She threw in a quick detail. "It is a pleasure cruiser, not a freighter."

"A pleasure cruiser docked in a marina? How are we supposed to sort through them all before it takes off?"

"Trust me, it won't be too hard." She looked at Doro and smiled. "I'm gonna drop the preacher off and meet you there."

"Once you do that," he reminded her, "your gig is complete. You should simply drop out and celebrate a job well done."

"I intend to celebrate," she informed him. "Dropping Doro off is the main course but I looked at the dessert menu and noticed an item called the Budria Butter-cream Surprise. I never leave a fine dining experience without enjoying dessert."

"If you beat me there, order mine with an extra cherry on top."

Agony stashed the phone in a pocket and snuck through a couple of corner store parking lots to avoid wasted time in having to wait behind traffic for a light to change.

"You never told me why you came for me," Doro ventured finally.

She looked at him for a moment, saw the kindness in his eyes, and shifted her gaze to the road again.

"Your congregation hired me to find you. Some thought you were probably dead and others held faith that you were still alive. They needed to know—oh," she remembered, "I am very sorry about your co-worker and church member who died to save you. He must have loved you very much."

"He loved everyone very much." He accepted her condolences. "Now, he is in the arms of God and helping God to do the same."

Agony reached the edge of Doro's neighborhood and he pointed out a street corner where she could drop him.

"This is close enough," he told her. "You have a boat to catch. The angel Michael will have your back, sister Alicia. God will take care of all your other sides."

She watched him hobble down a street with small shops and open markets. It was only a matter of minutes before he was surrounded by a mob that was in danger of hugging him to death.

But he was right. She had a boat to catch and she put the Jeep in gear.

Ignoring his safe driving advice, she pulled her phone out and redialed Pain's number. He didn't answer and she applied serious pressure to the pedal on the right as she raced toward the marina.

CHAPTER SIXTEEN

Pain had difficulty remembering the last time he'd had this much relatively innocent fun. Of course, the Caddie's bulletproof windows would give out soon and once they did, any shots that came through had a chance of hitting his head. As hard as it was, it was still the most vulnerable part of his body.

He also had to consider the fact that he and his pursuers were drawing a fair amount of attention as they careened through the city streets.

Film at eleven.

Although he had harmed no civilians, the cars he had nudged off the road had destroyed the hot dog cart but hopefully not its vendor. Oh, and there was that little sidewalk episode where he had slowed enough to give the customers who were enjoying their outdoor lattes at the quaint little tables a chance to choose between their lattes or their lives as he'd rolled through. He'd tried to skip a few car lengths ahead of his pursuers before he swerved onto the street again, turned sharply left, and again was forced to stop behind a row of school buses.

That led to him making a sloppy backward Y-turn during which the rear end of the Caddie might have punched through a storefront window and scattered several mannequins' body parts across the store's floor. While they would need reassembling, the mannequins didn't feel a thing and at least the employees would have something to do to keep themselves busy for a while.

No, no, no, he heard one of the assistants say in his mind. *The blonde's head was on the sundress body. The brunette's head goes with the dress for success torso.*

The Y-turn completed, he headed in the direction he'd come from and scowled when he realized two pursuers had now parked to block his escape.

He split the difference and roared straight ahead. The Escalade battered the cars' front ends and they spun into the street and blocked even more traffic. He continued into a park and tried to avoid the paved walking and biking trails that meandered through it.

The only thing that caused him any regret was having to drive through a flock of geese that thought they had every right to wander across his path, knowing full well that everyone had to come to a complete stop as they honked and flapped their wings and took their own damn sweet time.

Pain didn't have the luxury of being able to take his sweet time. He didn't feel any thuds under his tires so he knew he hadn't run over any of them, but the geese-rescue associations might have a few wings that needed bandaging. With a wry grimace, he made a mental note to send some money to the ASPCA when he had a chance.

Finally, he reached an actual street, proud of himself for having driven through the grass at one point in the park to pass a group of cyclists rather than simply nudging them one by one out of his way. They were, after all, in a park and not out on the street. The cyclists had the moral high ground this time.

As he raced down the street, following the blue line on the GPS to the address of the marina he'd punched in, he noticed that he had missed a call on the Caddie's phone. He recognized it as Agony's number. The last he'd heard from her, she was on her way to drop the preacher off and they had agreed to meet at the marina where the Budria was docked and was about to scurry off.

They hadn't known each other very long but she hadn't struck him as someone who would back out on a date. Even though this could be the personification of the blind date from hell, he knew she would do her damndest to keep it.

When he focused on the blue GPS line again after it had recalculated his present location—which took a while because a shortcut through a park hadn't been programmed in—he saw that he was behind the ETA he hoped for. He accelerated as the phone rang, pressed the button, and didn't worry to check the caller ID.

"Speak!" he answered.

"About time, asshole," she responded. "What did you do? Stop for a latte?"

"Something like that, yeah. What's your twenty?"

"The preacher is home and the gig is successful. I'm on my way to the marina now."

"ETA?"

"Probably sooner than yours. I'm not the type of gal to wait too long for her date to arrive before I start to party."

"Hold off on the fun as long as you can." He doubted that she would, of course. "I have to stop and pick up a tuxedo first."

"Don't forget the boutonniere." The line clicked and she was gone.

"Shit!" He slapped the dashboard in frustration. "She should have dropped the preacher off, called her gig complete, and gone home. The Budria is not her problem." Then again, it wasn't something he had signed up for either. A psychiatrist could send their kids to Harvard on the money they would have to pay to diagnose their psychoses.

Stay righteous, the voice from his past said. *Sure, Chaz,* he answered. *It's easy for you to say.*

He tried to focus on the marina but Chaz wouldn't leave his head alone.

Bishop to K-4. Your queen is now exposed.

I won't give this queen up. He was firm on that.

And you didn't give up on me!

For the umpteenth time, Pain heard his late partner's voice try to ease his conscience. Chaz hadn't succeeded yet but the man didn't have a stop nagging button. He sighed and continued his rush to reach the marina in the shortest possible time.

The city's serve and protect forces were busy attending to the damage he and his pursuers had left in their wake so there was no one left to keep track of whatever future mayhem might occur.

All that he had was a shot-up Caddie with a GPS that would lead him to the Budria.

Unfortunately, the bad guys had a GPS in the Caddie that would make him easy to track and possibly the knowledge of where the Budria was. If so, they probably already knew where he was headed. Oh, he reminded himself, and a shit-load of guns.

All his gear was in the subbasement of the Imperial Palace. As he streaked through the streets, he searched the Caddie for useful objects—a couple of half-empty bottles of water in the cup holders, a pair of Ray-bans hanging from the passenger-side sun visor, and an electric garage door opener clipped to the visor in front of him. It wasn't much to work with, even for him.

He also knew that Agony wouldn't have much to work with either if she beat him to the Budria—a long coat weighed down with confiscated handguns and a flip-baton. As good as she was, she would be seriously out-manned and out-gunned. Not that it would prevent her from trying to stop a boatload of terrorists from escaping, regardless of the odds. That was the kind of righteous bitch she was. He had to get there. Even if they failed, they'd at least have a puncher's chance for a knockout blow.

Despite all his evasive maneuvers, he was forced to stop with squealing tires when six cars blocked his forward path. This time, they had positioned themselves so there was no way he could simply bulldoze through them and go on his merry way.

In the rearview mirror, he saw six more lined up in the same formation. He was in the middle of a four-lane overpass, so a right-zig or a left-zag was not an option. Neither was surrender. At the marina, a bitch was about to head into an unpredictable situation with a group of desperate terrorists, whether he was there beside her or not. He didn't pray to God because he never held conversations with anyone he had never met face to face. But he did give a shout-out to the preacher, Doro, to put in a good word for him. He was not about to lose another partner to die on the deck of a boat and tumble overboard into the water. Having one partner buried at sea was enough.

Pain knew there was a pistol in the console of the Caddie behind the water bottles. He also knew that a loaded shotgun rested on the back seat.

His face pulled into a scowl. He didn't want to be the junkie who had finally gotten clean enough to be able to walk past a street dealer, only to turn back half a block later holding a folded twenty in his hand to make a smooth transaction with no words spoken and only a quick exchange of goods. But he wouldn't leave her to die alone.

If he had taken the time to pull the sun visor down, he could have checked his expression in the small mirror and would have looked upon a face that even Michael, the fighting archangel, might have had second thoughts about taking on. Doing something he had hoped he would never have to do again, he pulled a tube that was no bigger than a travel-sized tube of toothpaste out of a flap on his pants and applied it to his fingers.

That done, he took the shotgun from the back seat and ripped the center console open. He felt the weight of the pistol in his hand the way a reformed alcoholic who was about to suffer a relapse would open a bottle of Jack and inhale the fumes before he took the first gulp.

With the shotgun in his left hand and the pistol in his right, he said a silent prayer to Doro's God, asked for forgiveness for what he was about to do, and stepped out of the Caddie. He strode toward the cars behind him, kept his head in constant motion to avoid a lucky headshot, and trusted his bodysuit to take care of the rest of the barrage that would no doubt be directed at him.

Pain pulled the two shotgun triggers at the same time to fire both barrels. One man fell and another was left with a shredded arm that would never be able to fire a gun again, although he might be able to eventually handle a soup spoon.

He hurled the shotgun as if it were a Bowie knife and the stock split a forehead as he marched forward with the pistol toward where his recent victims had fallen. Still walking, he fired six rapid shots to eliminate five more of his adversaries and an innocent no passing on a double yellow line sign when someone ducked in time to avoid a bullet right between his eyes.

They retaliated and he dove into a double roll on the street below the slew of bullets aimed where his head had been. He scooped up the weapons of his first kills and fired sideways with both hands extended to direct one automatic stream of bullets to his left and one to his right.

He didn't hear the screams as the bullets found their marks. Now three cars deep into the rear six-car blockade, he fell prone on the pavement and fired the rounds he had left into the gas tanks of three of the vehicles.

It was purely a matter of time before a spark caused by a bullet striking metal ignited the stream of gasoline that poured onto the tarmac. First, one car was engulfed by the flames that roared into the sky. As the fire surged, a second followed immediately, and then a third as the entire scene in front of them erupted into an inferno that rose high enough to have melted any clouds that might have been hovering.

Out of this, those in the first blockade saw the Beast march out of the gates of hell. He leveled two more semis he had picked up along the way and without waiting for any backup demons, let loose.

Six of the twelve opposing him fell, never to rise again. The Beast had deadly aim. Two more took their best shots and he staggered for a moment before he continued to march forward and return fire.

Three more went down and the remaining three decided to take their chances. They ran and leapt over the overpass's guardrail. The screeching of brakes preceded a multi-car pile-up on the freeway beneath.

With no one left to fire at him, Pain surveyed the mayhem he had caused. His body quivered and he remembered why he had chosen to avoid firearms. They turned him into a man he did not want to be. He was so deadly with them that it didn't seem to matter how many foes he faced. It never felt like a fair fight. They also released an inner-self he was afraid would one day take over—one to whom the advice to stay righteous would sound quaint and antiquated. He wasn't sure whether loathing or fear was the more powerful emotion when he thought about that self.

He faced the line of cars in front of him that had stacked up behind his assailants' vehicles. They were between him and where Agony would be alone and outnumbered at the marina if he didn't get there on time.

His two immediate goals were to stop a terrorist plot and provide her with backup. The good news was that both objectives could be met at the same location. The bad news was that he had endured a five-minute delay and in a situation like this, that was an eternity. He dropped the guns he'd been holding. The goop from the toothpaste tube would obscure his fingerprints and he'd had enough of throwing death from a distance to last him for quite some time.

In the windshields of the cars ahead, he could see the reflection of the flames that still rose from the mayhem he had left behind him. The civilians were unable to move their cars either forward or back. He leapt onto the hood of the first one in line and ran over hoods, roofs, and trunks until he reached the last few cars in line, then jumped down alongside a Lexus—a convertible no less. This surprised him as he hadn't known that they made those anymore, but a flip-top always gave access to another escape route should one be needed.

He opened the driver's door, made sure no children were ducked down in the back seat, and informed the driver that he needed to borrow his ride.

The man left the engine running, snatched a briefcase from the passenger seat, and ran like hell as far toward the back of the line of the cars that continued to stack up behind him as he could.

Pain didn't blame him.

He slid quickly behind the wheel, made a U-turn, and raced down the street. Fortunately, his escape wasn't hindered by any emergency vehicles rushing to the scene, although he could hear sirens approaching in the distance. He no longer had a GPS at his disposal but he had memorized where the blue line had led and headed to the marina in what he hoped was the straightest line possible.

CHAPTER SEVENTEEN

Agony's phone rang and this time, she recognized the number.

"What's your ETA?" she asked without preamble.

"What's your twenty?"

"I asked first, Mister Late to the Party."

"Ten minutes," Pain answered. "Assuming no more wrong turns."

"The Caddie has GPS, moron. Please don't tell me that you have developed a sudden prejudice against modern technology that rivals your aversion to guns."

"I'm afraid the Caddie suffered a few fatal injuries but I gave it a land-locked equivalent of a Viking's funeral. I then upgraded to a Lexus—a convertible no less."

"I'm so happy for you." Her voice dripped with sarcasm the way water dripped over Niagara Falls.

"What's your twenty?" he repeated before he added, "Please don't make me ask a third time."

"There's only one road you can come in on and a traffic light where the road to the actual marina forms a T. At that light is a Gas and Grub. I'm in the parking lot doing the surveillance thing us former cops do so well."

"What are you driving?"

"A Jeep."

"All right." Pain remembered their last commandeering of vehicles. "You win the practicality round this time and I win the style points. Don't do anything stupid before I can get there."

"Why?" she retorted. "Have you reached a new level of stupidity you want to show me?"

"Oh, lady, you have no idea how high my level of stupidity can go."

She wanted to snap a sarcastic response but realized that he was probably right. "Just get here."

Eight minutes later—two minutes under his estimate—a silver Lexus with the top down skidded to a stop next to her. He leapt out without bothering with the door and she met him outside the Jeep and immediately noticed a few more bullet holes in his shirt and possibly some scorching of his eyebrows. She touched the one that seemed the worst off and sure enough, it didn't have much hair left.

"I got a little too close to some flames," was his only explanation.

"It gives a whole new definition to the uni-brow look."

"So, what do we have?" he asked as he surveyed the marina.

"The feds dropped the prisoner off five minutes ago."

"Are you sure they were feds?"

"They certainly weren't Boy Scouts and all their shoes were shined to within an inch of their lives."

That sounded like feds so he didn't argue. "Where are they now?"

"They handed him off to a group of four and scurried away. I think they were trying to avoid any undue attention."

"Gee, I wonder why they would want to do that?"

"I thought about calling in the Port Authorities," Agony continued, "but since the police have not confirmed any threat and the feds don't want to admit to any involvement, all that would have happened would be—maybe—a couple of agents not specifically trained in how to deal with terrorists would have arrived and asked a few questions."

"Questions about who?" Pain could envision the scene. "We don't even know the fucker's name."

"My thoughts exactly," she agreed. Somehow, throughout all their interactions with the terrorists, they had neglected to discover the main bastard's actual identity. "And if any of the questioning agents pushed too hard, they would have probably been shot and dumped in the water. I don't think these guys want to kill time hanging out here when they have an escape they want to hurry along."

"Have you come up with any plans yet?" His gaze scoured the marina.

"None that don't involve a shoot-out that could endanger dozens of hard-working fishermen."

"Where are they now?"

"They had reached their boat and boarded when you pulled up."

"Which boat?"

"Take a guess, Sherlock."

The Pleasant View Marina was not large. It was formed by two projections of land that curved into a circle, each side having a short berm at its end where boats coming in and out would pass through a narrow passage. In the center of this, a pole rose out of the water with a red light on top. Each berm also sported posts on them with green lights on the top.

Boats exiting the marina would keep the red light on their left and the green light on their right. Boats entering would do the same, forming two clearly marked entrance and exit lanes. It wasn't hard for Pain to locate the FA Budria. It was the only boat in the marina that wasn't weather-worn from daily trips on the water to bring in the fishermen's daily catch.

The vessel was bright white with one main deck, on top of

which was the command tower or pilot's cabin or whatever the fuck it was called. It rode high in the water. He guessed there were several no doubt luxurious living quarters located below.

"It's still docked," he observed. "We don't know his name but do you remember what the prisoner wore?"

"He's about five-ten and a little chunky," she recalled. "Black hair, black pants, and a black shirt—oh, and a shiny silver belt."

"He ought to be easy enough to identify." He studied the boat on which only a handful of crewmen were visible above deck, none of them close to being confused with a Nigerian. This confirmed their suspicions about the black-on-black gang warfare being a smokescreen.

"Maybe I can take a dive and try to scuttle it from below. I have a couple of waterproof plastic explosives that would do the trick. I merely have to get in the water beneath it to apply them."

"Aargh, Blackbeard." Agony growled in her best angry pirate's voice. "No time for scuttling. The scallywags are casting off now." She turned to face him with a scowl and added, "We scuttle it and then what? Try to negotiate a peaceful surrender? Whatever happened to we don't negotiate with terrorists?"

"I tried negotiating," he answered in a voice she thought sounded a little shaken.

"And?"

"And it didn't go well for the people on the other side of the table. But that was on dry land. Maybe negotiations at sea go a little more smoothly."

"Are you willing to bet your life on it?" She tried to decipher his tone.

"Mine? Yes." He made an effort to snap back to their current reality. "Yours? No."

She accepted the sincerity of his concern and felt touched.

They watched as the Budria cast off. A long line of fishing boats returning from their early morning forays waited to enter the marina while a shorter line of boats navigated out slowly between the red light in the center and the green light at the jut of the berm.

The pleasure cruiser positioned itself fourth in line.

"If I time it right," he said as his mind improvised a plan, "I can hit the end of the berm as the Budria passes. There's a green light there, right? And green always means go."

"So what, exactly," she asked in the interests of clarification, "is this particular level of your patented stupidity telling you to do?"

"If I time it right," he continued thoughtfully as he envisaged the scene, "I can land the Lexus in the captain's tower. That should ruin the day of whoever's in it and force a definite slow-down in their escape voyage plans."

"Or," she pointed out, "you could miss-time it and bounce across the deck and into the ocean."

"That's always a possibility," he admitted, "but I have a convertible with the roof down, so all I have to do is float to the top as the car sinks. I can swim, you know."

"Or," she responded to point out another flaw in the plan, "if the distance between the berm and the boat is too far, gravity and lack of speed might make you miss the deck completely and crash directly into the side of the boat."

"I never said the plan didn't have any flaws." He sounded defensive. "But either way, they won't be able to reach the high seas."

Agony replied with a throat-slashing motion and took a few steps away as she pressed a speed-dial number she hadn't used in a year or two. She hoped the bastard hadn't changed his number and neglected to inform her.

"Harry T," an impatient voice answered. "Don't waste my time."

"Two bodies in a shallow grave, off to the side of a walking trail through a park that was written off by the cops as a suicide pact."

"A-Gone-ee," Harry Tribelescheau responded. "Who, when, where, what, and why?"

"Get one of some news channel's choppers to the Peasant's View Marina pronto. Chaos is about to ensue. If I live through it, you will be able to put all the talking heads to shame when I give you an exclusive. The marina is only a scratch on the surface. There's deep shit on this one, Harry. Federal-level deep shit."

"And you're asking me to give the camera toters the first crack at it?"

"They'll owe you big time for informing them to be the first on the scene. Let 'em film and make wild guesses. This story has legs with a capital L."

"If you want me to give the pretty boys first dibs"—Harry sounded sincerely pissed off at the notion—"you'd better damn well live long enough to give me the exclusive."

"I love you too."

As far as she was concerned, Harry T was one of the last living, true-blue, wild-haired, constitution-kissing investigative journalistic assholes left on a planet. He'd once told her, "On the seventh day, God rested. On the eighth day, God woke up and said, 'Whoops, maybe I should have saved that Adam and Eve couple for another planet. They're not ready to populate one of their own yet.'"

She knew he would never stop digging if he thought a story was being buried by political machinations. Now was not the time to explain all of that to Pain, however. She hung up and strode toward the Lexus.

"You're about to press the pedal on the right with maximum force, aren't you?" she asked.

"Well…" He looked at her as if she had asked the dumbest question since Adam asked Eve if it was a sweet apple or a sour apple before he took a bite out of it. "It would be easy enough to find a brick or a stick to do that but who will drive the damn thing and be able to make adjustments for wind speed and other variables?"

Back to back Adam and Eve thoughts with two different indepen-dent sources? She shook her head and half-expected to hear cathedral bells ringing to announce that Sunday services were about to begin.

Agony discovered a sudden appreciation for convertibles as she vaulted over the door and slid into the shotgun seat as if it was a second skin.

"What?" he asked her. "No seat belt?"

"I'll take my chances." She pointed forward. "And by the way, I know how to swim too. Now floor it, bitch."

Pain laughed. "I thought you'd never ask."

He accelerated the Lexus out of the Gas and Grub and down the road to the marina, aiming for the berm on the right.

"Too fast—too fast!" she shouted. "We want the fourth boat out, not the third!"

"Maybe you should talk to the brick-stick on the pedal." He slowed a tad as he raced along the berm, cut the curve at the right speed, and with a slight fishtail, accelerated sharply before he shouted, "Shore to ship, permission to board!"

The berm's slight incline where the green light pole was located boosted the vehicle's elevation angle and it struck the Budria's command center's tower dead on.

Whoever was piloting the vessel at the moment of impact would not have had a chance to respond, even if he'd heard the request to board as a car made impact. To be fair, few boat pilots were trained to handle such an occurrence.

Those below deck didn't need to hear an announcement to know that something had gone seriously wrong with their smoothly planned and bartered escape. They had heard a loud collision from above that interrupted several self-congratulatory conversations, but the Budria didn't tilt to either starboard or port so it didn't cause them too much concern. What did worry them was that the boat didn't seem to be moving in any direction at all.

"Well now." Jeremy turned to his son as they were coming home from their morning catch and looked past the red-light buoy at the outgoing lane. "That's not something you see every day."

"No sirree!" his son Daniel replied. "I gotta get some pics."

"Of course you do," his dad agreed. "This time, you might be right."

He was proud of his teenage son who, every summer, rose out of bed each day before the sun broke the horizon to work as a fisherman. At the age of sixteen, the boy had calluses on his hands that might fade over time if he saved enough money to send his boy off to college, so he was not about to deny Daniel a simple pleasure.

Jeremy used the Internet only to keep track of the weather and the current prices on seafood so he would know where to set bait or cast nets. But he knew his son was fairly active on what he had called social media platforms, so these photos he snapped off would probably be impressive when his friends saw them.

Over time, his photos earned him a pretty penny when they went viral as the first ones taken at the scene of a Lexus convertible parked in the center of a pleasure boat's control tower. He was also invited to appear on several local morning news shows.

As the story gained traction, the hard-working teenaged son of a hard-scrabble fisherman even made it onto a couple of national shows. The boy had a lean body, a camera-friendly smile, and an easy-going charm. He could also tell a good tale and for a few weeks, his family and friends would gather together for a viewing party whenever he made an appearance on the TV.

When the new school year started, he was unanimously voted as his high school's Homecoming King and was the envy of every boy there for how much time he got to spend with the Homecoming Queen, Amber Sullucci—although it did earn him the eternal wrath of Brad Athmos, the star quarterback and Amber's boyfriend.

"Abandon car!" Pain shouted.

"Aye, aye, Captain!" Agony yelled in response.

They scrambled out of the convertible and onto the deck ten feet below in simultaneous drop and rolls.

"Don't shoot the last one to come out!" he hollered as he gained his feet and made a quick scan, looking for a belaying pin or any other object to use as a weapon.

"Don't tell me how to do my job, Captain Ahab!" she hollered as she took cover and waited for someone to emerge from below.

He peered over the edge to watch several crewmen who must have been on deck when the Lexus had made its unexpected flight and landing trying to swim toward the land.

"Men overboard!" he shouted to her and pointed them out.

She frowned as they flailed in the water. "I guess they preferred abandoning ship to going down with the ship."

"They don't make sailors like they used to." He was saddened by the notion.

The weight of the Lexus finally made the Budria tilt to the starboard side. Not that anyone left below deck knew what starboard was but if they had enough knowledge of the terms, they might all be wishing for a bottle of port.

There were two dozen plus one men below deck and each of them now scrabbled for their weapons.

"You stay here," one of the terrorists ordered the man in black.

"If I stay and the boat goes down," he replied, "Am I supposed to stay long enough to drown?"

"Just fucking stay for now!" the other man commanded as he

motioned to his men. "Conrad, George, follow me. The rest of you open the back hatch and get ready to get him and yourselves up and out of it."

"You got it, Peter," the second in command responded.

The leader was the first one to emerge but wasn't shot by Agony. Instead, his neck was suddenly encased by part of the ship's old-fashioned wooden steering wheel that fell from above. He dropped his gun and grasped the wheel to try to free himself, which gave Pain the split second he needed to lift him off his feet and hurl him over the rails.

From their vantage point on the stairs, Conrad and George didn't see the steering wheel. All they saw was Peter leaping off to the side of the opening with no shots having been fired. Interpreting this to mean that the coast must be clear, they rushed up.

Agony gave the next two to emerge enough time to step away from the stairs before she fired a shot at each and spun them to the side.

She faced Pain as they stood on opposite sides of the open staircase.

"I swear," she warned him in almost a hiss, "that if you holler Olly olly oxen free, my next shot will go right between what's left of your eyebrows."

"Fine." He threw up his hands, each one now holding a belaying pin, and backed away. "I weep for the fun you missed out on as a child."

They both had to adjust their stances hastily as the Lexus Effect finally took full hold and the Budria dipped dangerously on the starboard side. The ship angled sharply to starboard, which put it on a collision course with the berm.

The ocean didn't need the assistance of any functioning motor on a ship to propel it forward. A strong incoming tide swept the vessel relentlessly toward the shore.

Those below deck didn't know or care about the tides. All they knew was that two shots had been fired on the deck and no one had bothered to inform them that the coast was clear. They also knew the boat was suddenly tilted in a way that what was once the solid floor beneath their feet might turn into a wall soon. If that continued, they might all soon find themselves dancing on the ceiling.

Having not heard from Peter, the second in command, Nathaniel Carrington Worthington III, wasn't quite sure what his next order should be.

He had only joined the terrorist group because he was a spoiled trust-fund baby whose parents had always treated their only child as more of an ornament than their flesh and blood. His nannies knew that his favorite color was blue but he doubted that his parents did. To them, the only color that mattered was green.

Bored with the Ivy League college he had been sentenced to, he couldn't think of a better way to piss off his money-loving parental units than to join and help to fund a gang that wanted nothing more than to teach the fucking capitalists a lesson they wouldn't soon forget. Now, he was left on a sinking boat with two dozen eyes on him.

"If I may?" One of the terrorists he only knew as Sledge spoke.

NCW III nodded his permission to speak.

"Everyone, scramble up the steps and shoot at anything that moves." Sledge was firm. "There is only one person here on the Titanic that matters, and I will get him out of the hatch and onto shore and out of this clusterfuck. That is our only goal."

All that they knew about the man was that he was a former Marine and thought the rest of them were nothing more than momma's boys playing at being toy soldiers.

A sudden group consciousness took over and they rushed up the tilted stairs, determined to prove the Marine wrong in his evaluation of them.

Sledge frowned as they began to scramble up the stairs and turned to the pudgy man in black. "You'd better be worth it, motherfucker."

He grasped the man's shirt collar, hauled him to the back and up the short stairs, and opened the aft hatch. When he peered out, he saw they were now at a forty-five-degree angle to the water but land was only fifty feet away and closing.

"Can you swim?" he asked the bomb-maker.

"No. But I am an excellent floater."

Without a word, Sledge dragged the man up and out of the hatch and flung him into the water. Uttering every curse he had learned while in the Marines and then some, he dove in and managed to keep his charge's head above water as he fought through the tide toward dry land.

CHAPTER EIGHTEEN

Having dispatched the first three up the stairs in short order, Pain and Agony regained their balance on the tilting boat and managed to scramble back together, more on their hands and knees than walking steadily.

They met in a pile of rubble and kept it between them and the stairs that led below deck, where they expected the next line of resistance to come from.

"Sshhh," Pain whispered as he put a finger to his lips.

"Don't you tell me whether I should sshhh or not," she snapped.

He didn't bother to reply but he left her and slid across the wet and tilted deck until he was above the below-deck door.

With a finger in one ear, he tilted his head so his other ear was angled at the conversations taking place within. She had no idea what he heard and he could only make out part of it himself, but he'd heard enough rumbling and shuffling of bodies below to be able to look at her and flash his free hand in the air four times with the fingers splayed.

At least twenty still down below. She nodded, having understood the information.

Fuck, Pain thought as he caught another part of the conversation. *There is a back escape hatch? Everything else will be nothing more than a diversion.*

He slid and crab-walked to her across the seriously tilting deck.

"The man in black," he told her, "is going out through a back hatch—" That was all he was able to get out as the pilot's tower decided it was time to succumb to the inevitable. It fell and brought the Lexus with it.

They grabbed and pushed off of any solid object they could find and scrambled backward as the tower and the Lexus landed between them and the stairs. The deck of the Budria took it all in stride and continued with its tide-swept course toward its collision with the end of the berm.

The first of the terrorists reached the top of the stairs with Nathaniel Carrington Worthington III shouting encouragement as he rushed up behind him, finally ready to prove his worth. Cautiously, the man in the lead stepped out, ready to rain fire on anyone who opposed them.

Raining fire was one thing. Being able to rain a ton-and-a-half automobile left them thinking they might be a little out-gunned.

"At least it wasn't a Hummer!" someone shouted. "They ain't got shit!"

"They ain't got no shit like our shit," another voice called and the almost two dozen true believers—and Nathaniel Carrington Worthington III—scrambled up the ladder and onto the deck, stumbling and slipping all the way.

"You gotta admire their spirit," Pain acknowledged from the other side of the ruined tower and the poor innocent Lexus that had served them so well.

"Spirit, yes." Agony still tried to find solid footing. "Intentions, no. You flashed me twenty?"

"It was a rough guess," he conceded. "but it's all a diversion. Our target will try to slip out the back and swim to shore."

"Well then..." She checked what pistols she had left in her coat, not knowing how many rounds any of them held. "We ought to try to be there to greet him."

"I count twenty against two," he observed calmly.

"Never bet against the underdog." She opened fire and he went into action.

The terrorists also opened fire. The problem was that their only target practice had been held at firing ranges where the ground was always firm beneath their feet and the targets were nothing more than silhouettes pinned to a line or tacked to a bullet-stopping background. They had also always been stationary and had never once fired back. Nothing about their training was now relevant. The shooters' footing was anything but solid, their targets seemed to have no inclination to remain stationary, and for some unexplainable reason, were firing in return.

Agony was close to being seriously pissed off. She had dropped three but the boat now tilted at such a severe angle that she had to use one hand to hold onto whatever she could find to not slide into the water while she fired with her other hand. When that gun was out of rounds, she had to fish through her pockets with her free hand to find another with which to fire at targets who slipped and slid all along the sloping deck.

She caught a glimpse of her partner and remembered the first time he had pissed her off. He now seemed determined to do it again.

Bullets streaked left, right, and center from the emerging terrorists, who shot blindly as they dove and looked for cover. Chaos ensued but he seemed to be having the time of his life. He threw what looked like a weather-worn bowling pin at one of the terrorists' heads, made a direct strike, and slid across the tilting deck to catch his impromptu weapon as it tumbled. Without so much as a pause, he used it to good effect on the kneecaps of two others.

He then had the audacity to look at her and shout, "What are you waiting for, Ms. MMA?"

If she had been an old west gunslinger, she would have taken that as an invitation to "draw down," or perhaps to "sling it, sharpshooter," but she wasn't. Annie Oakley could do things with a gun that she would never be able to do. But Ms. Oakley wasn't there on this tilting, sinking ship and she, trained in MMA, was.

Any shots fired at them were more likely to kill a seagull than they were her or Pain. Her return fire produced similar results. It was time to get up close and personal until the Budria ran aground.

"I'll meet you on land, Blackbeard," she shouted.

"Yeah, I'll meet you there," he responded, "Queen of the Lowland Seas."

He threw another of his bowling pins and a lucky bounce ricocheted it from one head to another. Both men fell to their knees and the tilt of the Budria slid them into the water.

Another two down, she thought. *Twelve more to go.*

Agony found enough footing to be able to launch herself around the wreckage of the pilot's tower and the Lexus and into the rail on the high side of the boat. She kicked off the rail and twisted her body so she could slide and drive her feet into two terrorists' knees. The joints bent in a way knees were never meant to bend.

They screamed and clutched their knees as they slid helplessly down the Budria's tilting deck and under the pathetic excuse of a side rail into the water. The last two men to reach the deck scanned the scene and decided that maybe an exit through the back hatch wouldn't be such a bad idea. They shoved Mr. Moneybags down the stairs and dragged him along as they hurried as carefully as they could across the floor that was now tilted at a forty-five-degree angle.

"But I want to go down fighting!" NCW the III shouted.

"And we want to keep you alive," the terrorist in front, known only as Ricky, replied.

Nathaniel Carrington Worthington III was touched by their concern until the one behind him—whose name he thought was either Max, Mack, or Matt—added, "If we get out of here, we'll need your money to carry on with the mission. If we don't escape and are caught, we can use you as a hostage. Either way, you are coming with us."

Although that announcement destroyed any of the warm, fuzzy feelings he had momentarily felt because he thought someone cared about him, he could hear gunfire and screams from the deck and decided to take advantage of any assistance that was currently available.

The terrorists continued to fire, although half of them did so blindly because smoke now issued from the Lexus' engine and obscured their targets. Pain had one hand on the rail that was now on the high side of the boat and studied the scene.

Agony had decided to give up on her guns and attempts to stand upright. Instead, she propelled herself along the tilted deck and bounced from one terrorist to another.

Barely visible through the smoke, she used leg-swipes on those who were still semi-upright to bring them to her level and then used furious combinations of fists, elbows, and a head-butt or two. She then used the leverage of her most recently vanquished opponent to kick off and aim for her next target.

Pain saw something he didn't like and smelled something he liked even less. The Lexus had begun to slide slowly toward the rail she currently used to reach her next victim. Worse, he could smell the rubber burning from inside the engine and knew that a gas line was about to be left exposed.

After a pause to confirm the angle he was about to take and the direction he wanted to go in after his assault, he hurled himself feet-first and aimed his size fourteens at the chests of two terrorists who were crouched side by side. He felt the satisfying crunch of ribs as both feet made solid contact and used the momentum to kick off in Agony's direction.

Like everyone else, she now had difficulty seeing anything through the smoke and wiped her eyes before she tried to locate her next target. The one thing she hadn't expected was an attack from above, which was the only reason he was able to surprise her when he landed on the deck directly behind her.

She spun and stood face to face with him as he shouted, "You'll thank me for this later."

He braced his feet against one of the guardrail posts, stood at an odd angle, and grasped the shoulders of her long coat to heave her as high and far into the water as he could before he dove in after her.

When she pushed through the surface, sputtering and spitting water, the asshole was treading water right in front of her.

"What the fuck was that all about?" she managed to say before the Lexus' gas tank exploded and he shoved her head underwater. He dragged her away from the explosion.

When they finally emerged again, the vehicle was now in the water and flames still climbed as a mixture of oil and gas began to spread across the calm marina's surface.

"You said you could swim, right?" he asked as she kicked slowly to stay afloat.

"Not while wearing the coat, asshole."

"I warned you about carrying all that extra weight in its pockets."

"Fine time for a lecture, Dad."

"Then don't!" He smiled.

"Don't what?" She hated it when his smile took on such smugness.

"Don't try to swim."

"You're advising me to sink and grow gills?"

He shook his head. "I'm advising you to stand. We're only in four feet of water and can scramble onto the bank from here."

Agony shoved his chest, which felt as solid as if she had pushed against a mountain, and used the counter-force momentum to fight to the edge of the berm and scrabble to the top. She stood and he joined her seconds later to look toward the Budria.

The water was now on fire and the Lexus sank slowly. It was obvious that the boat would never set sail again when the flames began to engulf it. They could hear the screams of several terrorists still in the water while a handful of others were able to reach the berm's bank and now dragged themselves up its side.

"You're welcome," he said as he scanned farther down the berm.

"Thank you," she replied grudgingly and shook the water out of her short hair.

Pain stepped back and wasn't sure whether to laugh or ask what the fuck she thought she was doing.

She hopped up and down on one foot and tilted her head at a right-side-down angle while simultaneously pounding the left side of her head.

A moment later, she switched feet, tilted her head in the opposite angle, and repeated the same procedure.

"If this is some type of a ceremonial dance," he ventured, "it is one that I am not familiar with."

"I have sensitive ear canals, okay?" she responded, her dance now done. "They don't like having water in them."

"Oh." He was in serious danger of laughing. "Then maybe the next time you tell me 'I can swim too, now drive, bitch,' you should make sure you have your earplugs handy."

"Feel free to make fun of me later all you want at your own risk, but for now, where is Mister Silver Belt?"

"I think he and his last-line of protection defender are coming out of the water now, about a hundred yards down."

"Do you have any more jests at my expense or can we finish this now?"

"Jests later." He smiled. "I'll need time to come up with more." His expression turned serious. "Let's be done with this fucker."

They had to fight through a dozen terrorists who had managed to reach land before they had and now stood on the flat, paved surface on the top of the berm. While the men reached for their water-logged guns, the two partners didn't worry about who might or might not be able to fire at them. They also didn't want to leave anyone still on the surface who could shoot at them from behind.

Pain wanted to lead the charge since his bodysuit was better able to take bullets than Agony's unprotected body could, but she decided to take the ladies first approach. He therefore followed in her wake as she threw palm-smacks and delivered chops to heads and hard surfaces and fisted blows to softer tissues. He had to admire her technique.

"Not bad for a girl," he shouted as he tossed the bodies she'd pummeled into the water. She took a moment to spin and give him a double middle-fingered salute.

Her sass came partially from the fact that she'd dispatched a scrawny little terrorist simply by looking deep into his eyes. The guy took one look and glanced behind her before he leapt voluntarily into the water. When she turned, she faced a terrorist who was bigger than Pain and six inches wider.

He had a very ugly smile and an even less attractive look in his eyes as he motioned her forward.

"You're not dealing with an amateur now, bitch." He snarled a challenge.

"Neither are you."

Agony launched herself into a right-footed kick at his head, which he ducked easily, but her left foot pounded into his ugly smile and made mincemeat of his nose. She landed flat on her back in a trained fall and swept his legs out from under him with a swiping kick at his ankles.

She bounded to her feet and turned to her partner. "I think I've softened him up enough now for you to be able to handle him."

"I'm almost impressed," Pain said as he joined her above the man who tried to stand. He grasped the back of the giant's shirt to hurl him into the water. The garment gave way before the giant's body did and he was left holding a handful of polyester.

"Shit!" he muttered. "Cheap terrorists and even cheaper clothes."

He delivered a quick kick to the giant's face in case Agony had missed anything, then stood to the side and put a boot to the asshole's ribs to give him a not so gentle nudge into the water.

"Not bad for a girl?" She faced him.

Pain shrugged, "What can I say? I've never been good at pep talks."

They turned to rush after the man with the silver belt and suddenly stood face to face with three men. Two of them had a hard look about them and the third, who had a much softer countenance, had a knife held to his throat by one of the others who stood behind him.

"Tell them your name," the man with the knife commanded.

"I am...I am...." the soft one stuttered.

"Your name, rich boy. Only your name." The knife-wielder seemed seriously desperate and pissed.

"I am Nathaniel Covington Worthington the Third." It emerged as a sputter, probably out of fear.

"We want a safe way out of this," the first man informed them, "or the rich boy dies."

"I got this." Pain took the lead and Agony stepped back since at this point, neither of them knew what was truth and what was fiction. All they knew was that their quarry with the silver belt was on the other side of these three and no doubt scurrying to an escape vehicle.

"So," her partner said, "we either arrange a way out for you or you slice his throat?"

"Exactly." The man smiled, sure that his demands were about to be met.

"But what if there is no throat for you to slash?"

He didn't give the terrorist any time to ponder the question and a ten-pointed star flew out of his hand and stuck the rich boy in the kneecap. He fell with a shriek.

The knife-wielder looked at his hostage, who writhed and held his knee, then at the big man in time for another ten-pointed star to lodge in his throat.

With a yelp of alarm, the third terrorist made a sensible decision to turn and run for his life.

Agony searched the fallen man and found one pistol that she tossed into the water. He still clutched his knee, where the star protruded.

"My name is Nathaniel Covington Worthington the Third," he whined.

"Did I ask you your name?" She yanked the star out and he shrieked before he continued. "No, but my parents are the Worthingtons. They will pay big money for my safe return."

"You mean *the* Worthingtons? The Mayflower Worthington descendants?"

He nodded vigorously. "Yes! Those Worthingtons."

"I've never heard of them." She rolled the useless twit's body toward the water and let him fend for himself before she turned to see Pain yank a star out of the other man's neck. He wiped it on the terrorist's clothing and slid it up his sleeve.

"I believe this is one of yours?" She handed him the Worthington star.

"Thank you," he said, wiped the second star down, and slid it up his sleeve to join God only knew how many others were lodged there. He nodded down the berm.

"Mr Silver Belt and friend, three hundred feet and moving."

With no more terrorists to hinder them, they raced forward. If their quarry managed to reach the parking lot, he and his accomplice would no doubt find a car. Fortunately, their presumed destination was nine hundred feet away and the man was pudgy and not used to physical exertion. They caught up to them eight hundred feet later.

When Sledge heard the running footsteps closing in—and tired of dragging the pudgy man along—he decided he'd had enough. He released his fellow escapee's sleeve and wasn't surprised when the man fell, gasping for breath. The terrorist turned and faced his pursuers.

"Two of you on your side," he said, "and only"—he looked at the man who was gasping for air and made a disgusted face—"and only one and a half on my side. But you do have to get through me to get to him."

For as many deaths as the terrorists had caused and however many more he and Agony were determined to prevent, Pain took a moment to admire his opponent. They were almost the same height and less than ten pounds separated them. The man's stance confirmed that he was ex-military. He made eye contact and nodded. No guns, just mano a mano.

"Keep an eye on the other one," he told Agony. "He is our only objective."

She had no time to argue as he and the man who seemed to be his equal approached each other, their hands raised at their sides as if to say neither of them was armed. That didn't mean she wasn't armed and ready to use her weapon if her partner went down.

The two big men ignored everything except each other and both stood sideways to prevent direct blows. They circled one another clockwise and spoke before the battle began, although she couldn't hear what they said.

"Pain." He introduced himself to his opponent. "Ex-damn near everything."

"Sledge," the man replied. "Ex-Marine."

"I guess we've both made a couple of wrong turns somewhere," he suggested as they continued to circle.

"At least one of us has," his opponent acknowledged and attacked first with a left-footed kick to his ribs. Pain raised his right arm rather than trying to block it and let his body armor absorb the blow, but the force of it still made him lean to his left.

Sledge is a lefty. His brain registered the thought but immediately reminded him that the man was probably capable of being ambidextrous if a situation called for it. He changed the circle's direction to counter-clockwise and threw two hard left-hand jabs that made a solid connection with his opponent's chin. The man staggered back half a step but came nowhere near falling from the strike.

The ex-Marine smiled at him. "That's the best you got?"

"Your opening salvo was a little weak too, bro." He returned the smile. "The power of any kick comes from the hips. You're a little out of practice, Marine."

Agony was both fascinated and distracted. She had drawn a pistol from one of her coat pockets that had a snap and hoped it had kept some of the water out to enable her to fire should Pain go down.

At the same time, she had to keep an eye on the pudgy man in case he managed to draw enough wind into his lungs to make a run for it. He merely remained seated and trusted his protector. *Also,* she thought wryly, *you have no idea which car to run to. The one that dropped you off drove out as soon as they could after they'd dropped your shit-ass off. Never think the feds are your friends.*

Having decided that he wasn't going anywhere anytime soon, Agony turned her attention to the fight in progress. The two trained professionals were now engaged in what could only be described as a two-man street brawl.

Close-contact elbows, head-butts, and arm yanking paused momentarily as each of them backed away and wiped the blood from their eyes. They stretched and flexed to verify which joints were still functioning before they continued. Sledge moved his left hand to his right shoulder.

Pain noticed the action. In their latest scuffle, he had yanked the arm hard and thought he felt the shoulder pop out of joint. He immediately dove, rolled, and came up to grasp his opponent's now useless right hand above the wrist.

There was no need to yank on it as a shoulder could only come so far out of joint, but he maintained a solid hold on it and spun as if he were an Olympian competing in a hammer toss.

Sledge's body, still attached to his shoulder, had no choice but to follow and splashed into the water ten feet away. The toss wouldn't have earned any medals for distance, but he would have earned a gold for effectiveness.

Pain, bruised and hurting, took no time to celebrate his victory over the Marine. Instead, he rushed to their quarry and ignored his partner as he leaned over the pudgy man and demanded, "What do you know about Treble Hook? Tell me now or I will pick you up, dive into the water with you, and drown you myself!"

"Then we'll both die," the bomb-maker retorted. "Me in the water and you in prison. If we both die now, only one of us will die knowing the truth behind Treble Hook and it won't be you."

"What the fuck is Treble Hook?" Agony demanded, nonplussed by this random subject when the dirty bomb had been at the forefront of her thoughts.

"Never mind," her partner snapped but refused to meet her eyes. "It doesn't concern you."

Sirens now screamed from a short distance away.

"Pain! Pain!" She tugged at him and shouted, "Sirens! We are on everyone's shit list right now. We won the battle. Now let's live long enough to win the war."

He wanted to shake her hand off and strangle the pudgy man, immediate consequences be damned, but she said the magic word. "This is not the place for your Quest to end."

Still, his driving instinct wanted to toss the pudgy man over his shoulder and run down the berm, past the marina's offices, and up the hill to where the Jeep was still parked at the Gas & Grub. More than anything, he wanted to question him further but Agony's strong hands yanked him back.

"Sirens and us," she shouted, "have never been a recipe for success."

Pain stood, gave the bomb-maker a solid kick below his belt buckle, and rushed after his partner to the parking lot of the Gas & Grub.

Seconds later, as the official cars with their sirens turned into the marina, she pulled out of the lot and drove as far from the scene as possible before any roadblocks could be set up.

CHAPTER NINETEEN

"I smell fish," Augusto Zaza stated in a raspy voice that was barely above a whisper. "I ordered rigatoni. It never has fish. Is the chef not aware of that?"

When he realized that he was speaking from a hospital bed without first pressing the nurse-call button, he looked at the corner of his room where his two bodyguards, Marco and Alphonse, were seated upright in their chairs, totally motionless with their eyes closed. Even through his hazy eyesight, a lifetime of violence had taught him to recognize death and he knew he wasn't looking at two dead men. He also knew they hadn't decided to both take a nap while on duty.

The Camorra leader had an innate aversion to hospitals, a trait he shared with ninety-nine point nine percent of the human population. The nurses were supposed to be at his beck and call, and when he pressed the call button and didn't get a quick enough response, he would send one of his guards out to personally escort one to his room. That was not a current possibility, so he fumbled frantically for the button but it wasn't where it was supposed to be.

Even if it had been, it might still take all of five minutes for a nurse to appear. He was used to someone appearing within seconds after he had summoned them. And doctors? Pah! All over, the doctors he knew had told him that he should have been dead five years earlier. What the fuck did they know? He closed his eyes, rested his head on the pillows, and wondered if he was maybe in a dream. The best way to get out of a dream, he'd long since learned, was to will himself out of it.

But the fall from his office window had taken a toll on his body. Not as big a toll, though, as it had taken on the youngster who had landed first on the sidewalk and cushioned the blow when Augusto had landed on top of him. He couldn't remember if he had ordered flowers for the funeral or not. The pain meds hooked up to his IV had muddled his brain, which might explain the dream he was having.

At least the pain-med button worked when he pressed it. He tried to not over-work it, though. That was the one thing he didn't want to be taken away from him. Pain in his body? Well, that was something that he had learned to separate himself from. It was simply pain, and could and should be ignored.

When he was much younger, a mentor had told him over a couple of glasses of fine red wine, "Augusto, you will eventually reach an age, if you live long enough, where you will wake up every day with one body part hurting more than the others."

"And what should I do then?" he had asked.

"Identify the part that hurts the most and do your best to ignore it for the rest of the day." His mentor had smiled as if it was the simplest advice he had ever given.

"But what about the other body parts that hurt?" he had asked. "What should I do with them?"

"Celebrate them," the man had replied after he had taken a sip of the warm red wine. "If you can feel pain, do you know what that tells you?"

"No, I don't." Augusto remembered the answer and wondered if it was the wine or dementia talking through his mentor's mouth, although the older man had never shown any signs of dementia or drunkenness before.

"If you can feel pain"—the man set his wine glass down and met his eyes—"you will know you are still alive. Dead men feel no pain."

"Fuck the pain." He reached for the button that led to the IV. "Pain I can deal with but peaceful sleep? I don't get that very often. And who the hell brought fish into my room?"

"That would be me." Zaza frowned at the unexpected voice. "Although I didn't bring the fish in so much as I brought the stink of them in. I hope you don't think any less of me for having done that."

Pain knew the old man's voice wasn't capable of calling out in anything louder than a whisper.

"You?" the Camorra leader managed to mutter at the demon who now loomed over him. He had appeared from hell itself and had thrown a body at him that had made him fall through a window. The incident had led to his current stay in a hospital bed at the mercy of incompetent doctors and sadistic nurses.

Zaza made the sign of the cross and rasped, "Be gone from me, Satan!"

"Wrong angel there, Zaza," Pain answered calmly. "I am the Archangel Michael. I am the one who kicked Lucifer's ass—or so I've been told." He winked at Agony when he recalled the preacher Doro's description of him.

She stood in a corner of the room out of the patient's sight and had to stick a fist in her mouth to stop herself from laughing as she waited her turn.

The old man was able to look past the devil to where his two men sat motionless in their chairs and understanding began to seep in. But he was Augusto Zaza, and even with a battered body and a muddled brain, he managed to swallow his fears and look the devil in the eye.

"If you intend to do it," he rasped through a mouth and throat that the medications always left feeling too dry, "then do it. I will not beg for my life. Men live and men die, but only cowards beg."

The man, who Zaza now realized was only a man and not a demon, smiled. It did not hold any warmth or sympathy and he knew deep down that if the big man so desired, he could turn him into a coward who was thoroughly capable of begging.

"That wasn't on my agenda today, Mr. Zaza," his unwelcome visitor replied. "But as you have your next conversation, please keep in mind that agendas can be very flexible. Oh, it seems you have a second visitor. I believe you know Ms. Goni, AKA the Butch Bitch."

Pain stepped into the background but still within Zaza's line of sight as Agony stepped into the light.

"Oh, Gus, Gus, Gus." She tssked, "What happened to you? Didn't anyone ever tell you that you can never win an argument with the ground? No matter how high you are when you throw yourself at it, the ground won't feel a thing."

She wiggled one of his toes that was exposed at the end of a foot cast. "Did this little piggy go to market?"

The old man uttered a short yelp.

"I guess maybe not." She gave it another slight wiggle. "This must be the one that went wee, wee, wee all the way home."

Zaza bit back another yelp and clenched his teeth for a moment. "I think I prefer the devil over there to you and your sadism. It was one of the youngsters, not me, who referred to you as the Butch Bitch. Although I am beginning to believe that his description was more accurate than my assessment of you."

"Then let's pretend." She pulled a chair closer and sat in it, out of easy reach of his piggly-wigglies. "Let's pretend that your assessment of me is the more accurate."

"I have always wanted to think so." He leaned back and stared at the ceiling. "I suppose you have control of my nurse-call button as well as my pain pump?"

In answer, she held both buttons up. "I came to you, Gus, to make a simple courtesy call to let you know that I would be nosing around in your territory and to assure you that it would have nothing to do with your operations. What should have been a short, straightforward conversation ended up with me facing a firing squad. That was no way to treat a lady."

"No," Zaza agreed. "It was very impolite of me."

"To say the least." She couldn't argue with him.

He lowered his gaze from the ceiling, focused on her, and gave her the closest thing to an apology he had given anyone in recent memory. "It was a business decision but perhaps it was an opportunity I should have declined. The reality, Ms. Goni, is that if I hadn't taken it, several others were waiting in line behind me."

"And that is why I am here, Augusto Zaza." She used his full name in an effort to show him the respect he felt he deserved. "There will probably never be peace between the Camorra and its thugs and me. Too much damage has been done for them to let that go. But I am willing to make my peace with you, one to one, if you can tell me who was behind the plan to issue a death warrant on me."

Zaza sighed. "If I say that I do not know, will you wiggle my toe until I make up a name?"

"If I believe you are telling me the truth, then no. Your toes will be safe from me."

With a touch of doubt and fear, he looked past her at the big man. "What happens if I convince you but do not convince him?"

Agony looked at Pain—who seemed to be using a fingernail to try to remove something from his front teeth—and faced the old man again. "If you don't convince him, he will probably bite off each of your toes, which will most likely cause excruciating pain."

"I do not doubt that he would." The Camorra leader was past the point of trying to bluster. "But sadly, as much as I would wish for peace between the two of us and as fond as I am of each of my toes, I do not know the answer to your question. I only spoke briefly to him and only once on the phone when he asked me if we would be interested. They would pay very handsomely and the payout would be arranged through a dead drop."

"You told me," she remembered, "that the person or group who took the contract out on me came from my side of the tracks, not yours. Why did you think that?"

"Do you think I don't know a cop's voice when I hear one?" Zaza scoffed. "Besides, you are no longer a cop and therefore no longer a threat to anyone on my side. Anyone who wanted revenge for your past actions would have preferred to exact it personally rather than farm it out."

Agony glanced at Pain, who'd heard what she had. "His toes are safe from me," was his short reply to her look.

She turned to Zaza and said, "La pace."

Zaza nodded, "La pace."

"For now," she added. "Next time? No guarantees."

"My prayer is that we have no next time. May I have my buttons back now?"

Agony gave the pain-med button three quick pumps and waited while the morphine kicked in. She believed he'd spoken the truth but wanted to make sure he was sleeping as peacefully as a man with so much blood on his hands could sleep before they headed out. He would wake up in an hour and that would give them enough time to put some distance between them and the hospital before he could sound any alarms.

———

Pain strolled to where Gus's bodyguards were still seated. He must have seen something he didn't like because he gave each of them a side-chop to the lower side of their necks. To her, it looked like the karate equivalent of the Vulcan nerve-pinch and she watched each body slump a little lower in its respective chair.

"Will you teach me that sometime?" she asked as they headed to the door.

"May I ask why?"

"Because I've been on a date or two before when I've had to excuse myself to use the little girls' room. A move like that would have left me with time to make my escape from boredom before I had to return and try to not vomit while I politely finished my entrée."

"Understood." He opened the door to Zaza's room and scanned the hallway. "You'll have a lot in common, they said, but the lot in common ended after it was established that we were both bipeds. We're clear. Elevator or stairs?"

"Stairs." She didn't hesitate. "Elevators are too confining and I don't like it when the only options to push are which floor or the emergency button."

He took her hand as if they were a couple who had visited a relative, walked calmly past the nurses' station, and gave them all his best smile as he moved toward the stairwell.

"Funny," he said as the happy but concerned couple made their way down the hallway. "You didn't express such reluctance about using elevators when we were on our way up here."

Agony swung her arm playfully, going along with the charade, and answered in a soft voice. "That's because we had just gotten here and Gus's room was on the sixth floor. But we've been here for over two hours now and who knows how many eyes have been on how many cameras since our little dust-up at the marina...my dear."

The happy couple entered the stairwell and hurried to the first floor and out through the lobby to the street. The four-level parking garage where the Jeep was on the third level was only a pedestrian crossing away.

"We could have found some street parking," Pain muttered, close to complaining, "if one of us had been willing to drive her recently acquired Jeep around a block or two."

"And then what?" Agony countered. "Have to come back every

two hours to feed the meter? How many quarters do you have in your pockets?"

"So the Jeep gets a ticket," he told her. "It's not like it was in your name."

They used the pedestrian cross-walk as calmly as any other couple would.

"When was the last time," he asked her, "that anything good happened in a parking garage?"

"One of us," she retorted, "has watched too many movies."

She headed to the elevator where she hit the button for Level Three.

"Oh." Pain joined her inside the enclosed space. "Now you are all in favor of elevators?"

"Will you, for once in your life, lighten the fuck up?"

"And will you," he responded, "for once in your life, show some consistency?"

"Fine!" Agony pressed the Level Two button that caused the elevator to make a sudden stop. The doors opened and she motioned for him to go first.

He complied and led the way to the stairwell to Level Three.

"And you think I'm the paranoid one," she muttered as she followed him up the stairs.

The stairway doors in parking garages had no windows, so Pain decided to hold back before he opened it. He was about to motion her down the stairs to ground level where they could find another vehicle, even if it was only a city bus, when she pushed past him and opened the door.

She stepped calmly through and he drew a deep breath and set his paranoia aside as he followed her onto the parking deck.

Fuck, he thought, *if I ever have a daughter, I will name her Para-noi-a. If I ever have a son, I will name him Paranoi-o and hope their names serve them well.*

Agony was holding her hands at her side but reached one of

them back to him. He took it and stepped forward to stand beside her.

"Now is not the time!" she whispered to him out of the side of her mouth.

"And why is that, my dear?" he whispered in return as he tried to keep his adrenaline down to a level that would still leave some of the bones in her hand resembling bones and not sawdust.

"Because," she replied calmly, "these people all seem to be friends of yours and at the moment, they have us seriously out-gunned."

"And you wonder why I prefer street parking."

He wanted to let go of her hand and inflict some serious damage, especially on the SISTER agent whose nose hadn't quite healed from Agony's blow to it when she'd followed them in her old company-provided beige sedan a few days earlier.

The young woman was now at the back of the formation. A dozen agents were in front of her and also stood between the Jeep they had hoped to hop into and scoot out in after their conversation with Augusto Gaza.

Agony had been right. They had stayed too long in one place.

Pain had been right. Parking garages sucked.

"It's your call." He gave her the choice for their next move, confident that between the two of them, they could fight their way out of the situation they were now confronted with.

"There is more than one way to fight," she reminded him. She held his arm tightly, pulled her cell out, and pressed speed-dial.

"Harry T. Don't waste my time."

She gave him their location and the parking garage level before adding, "Don't waste my time either, asshole. You have five minutes to get here with someone on your newspaper staff who knows how to operate a camera or you lose your exclusive."

"Give me six," he begged.

"I'll give you four." She ended the negotiation and hung up.

"What the fuck was that about?" Pain hadn't thought it was

the most appropriate time for her to choose to use a cell phone as a weapon.

"That," she informed him, "was how sometimes, patience can be a very valuable weapon and how sometimes, the pen can be mightier than the sword, especially if the pen has a photographer behind it."

"What the hell are you talking about?"

"We have two options. A firefight now that can be buried or a peaceful surrender by two people who have done nothing wrong. Or, at least, nothing that is provable." She nodded toward the dozen agents with twitchy fingers who no doubt waited for them to make one wrong move before they opened fire. "If your friends over there take us into custody—either dead or alive—without any witnesses…well then, I guess they win."

He surveyed the feds lined up against them. "And if I don't make any sudden moves?"

"Then all we have to do," she advised him, "is hem and haw for a few minutes until a third-party witness arrives. Are you or are you not capable of such a simple task?"

CHAPTER TWENTY

Pain pushed her away, stumbled toward a pillar, and thunked into it face-first. He staggered back with blood on his face and shouted, "The bitch got me drunk! I told her I couldn't handle the booze and what did she say? One margarita can't hurt you."

Agony won her self-bet over how soon he would change his first name again as she watched Margarita Pain perform. After he'd pounded his face into the pillar and accused her, he stumbled and face-planted on the floor. He rose onto his hands and knees, his face even bloodier, and pointed at her while he shouted, "Save the next round for your next boy-toy! Can someone—anyone—please help get me into rebibahab?"

Quizzical looks and silence were the responses of the agents with the guns who watched the spectacle. Encouraged, he pushed on in his role of a large, stumbling drunk when he attempted to stand and instead, fell flat on his back and mumbled, "Rehoo... No, no. Hoo hab... No, no...reboobihab."

The experienced agents looked at the young female agent who had tipped them off to this. The older agents were simple feds. She belonged to a whole different branch that was beyond their need-to-know orders. They looked from the stumbling drunk to her and she pulled her cell out and pressed a speed-dial button.

"My car is here somewhere." Still flat on his back, Pain held an open palm out. "All I need is the keys, please, and I can drive myself to...to...to whatever it'sh called. My car knows the way by heart."

The agent in charge had seen enough and finally decided to take charge. This was Agent Duncan Simmons' first AiC real-life assignment and he was trying to do his best to not fuck it up but no one made it easy for him.

"There are no keys." He stepped forward decisively and stood on one of the drunk's wrists while he stared at the young agent who had gotten them all into this.

In the silence, the elevator dinged and everyone adjusted their aim as the door opened.

"Hello hello hello!" Harry T shouted as a photographer hurried up behind him. "Does anyone want to give me a quote I can use?"

"Who the hell invited the press?" Agent Simmons raged as he stepped off of the big man's wrist and took a step toward the uninvited guest.

"That would be me." Agony raised a hand and confessed cheerfully.

Simmons spun. "And you are?"

"Not obligated to tell you." She followed this with her most innocent smile. "My mother always told me to never talk to strangers."

"I am not a stranger." He fumbled for his badge and held it out. "I am FBI Agent Duncan Simmons. I am in charge here and I asked you a direct question."

"Yes, you did." She nodded. "But that was before you produced any credentials."

"Duncan Simmons," Harry T interjected as he scribbled notes

and his photographer moved around, snapping away. "Simmons with two ems?"

"What the fuck does it matter how many ems there are?" The man spun to face Agony. "All right then, lady. I have now properly identified myself as an agent of the United States Government so I will ask you again, what is your name?"

"Alicia Goni, private investigator." She turned to Harry T. "That's Goni, G-O-N-I—many people get it wrong."

The reporter winked at her. She had been right. This was turning into quite a carnival.

"And who is your drunken son of a bitch boyfriend?" The agent seemed determined to let everyone know that he was in charge.

"First of all," she said frostily, "I don't have a boyfriend and am not looking for one in case you thought of asking me out later, Agent S-I-M-M-O-N-S. And as for some drunken son of a bitch, I have no idea who you are referring to."

AiC Simmons spun and pointed to where he'd left the big dope on the floor, but the idiot now leaned calmly against a pillar without a drop of blood on his chin or forehead.

"What the fuck are you doing?" the agent shouted.

"The pillar here felt a little wobbly," the big man answered without a trace of slurred speech. "I simply thought I'd help to support it for a few minutes while I enjoyed the show."

"This isn't a show, asshole. What's your name?"

"Mephistopheles Payne." He turned to Harry T. "That's P-A-Y-N-E. You'll have to Google how to spell Mephistopheles. I usually simply use my first initial."

"Reporter," Simmons ordered, "step back! Photographer, step back farther!"

"You do realize," Harry T informed the agent, "that he has multiple lenses."

"I don't care if he has multiple wives! I merely don't want you in the way while I place these two under arrest."

"On what charges?" Pain asked calmly as he clasped his hands behind his back while he continued to lean against the pillar. If they intended to cuff him, they would have to first move either his body or the pillar.

"We are the FBI." AiC Simmons realized that he had been shouting, brought his voice under control, and sneered. "We don't need charges. All we need is authorization."

"Okay, then." Pain could be a reasonable man. "Under whose authority?"

"Under hers, asshole." The man turned to point to the young female agent who had so far stayed in the background.

"Gosh." He almost felt sorry for the AiC. "I'm not sure which her you are referring to."

"Dammit!" Simmons still pointed at the empty space where she no longer stood. "Where did she go?"

His agents looked around and shrugged.

"I don't know sir," one of the agents replied. "Our eyes were trained on the suspects."

Pain, being one of the subjects, had no such restriction on his visual obligations and had seen her retreat quietly and make her exit once she realized that things would not go her and SISTER's way.

"All right, then." Simmons turned to him again. "Then under my authority. Agent Duncan Simmons, the FBI is taking you into custody for questioning regarding a wide-ranging investigation."

The partners knew this was all now merely bluff and bluster on the AiC's part but decided to give the poor man a break. They stepped forward.

"No cuffs," Pain said calmly, "and we will come peacefully."

Simmons thought about how hard it would be to cuff the big man, especially with the fucking photographer still snapping away, and nodded.

"No cuffs," he conceded.

"And no separate vehicles," Agony demanded. "If we don't go together, we go nowhere."

That was one demand too many for the AiC, but right then, three city squad cars squealed into the garage. An obvious veteran of the force stepped out of the lead vehicle and held his badge up.

"Sergeant Ishmael Jeffries," he announced. "These two are wanted for questioning in a series of possible 4-31's."

"My badge outranks your badge, Sergeant Jeffries," the agent scoffed as he held his fed credentials out. "But feel free to tag along and you can have what's left of them once we're done."

Thanks to her partner's very effective distraction, no one had noticed Agony make a second phone call. She had convinced whoever had answered the Cube Nine phone that she was one of Sergeant Jeffries' confidential informers and needed to speak to him ASAP.

He was on the phone within ten seconds and in a lead squad car two minutes later, en route to the parking garage. Unperturbed, he approached the fed and verified the badge the man held out.

Knowing that he had now provided Agony with enough backup to ensure that the feds didn't somehow lose their suspects while on the way in for questioning, he took a step back and bowed gracefully.

"You lead, Agent Simmons, and we will be honored to follow in your most inestimably inconsequential wake."

The AiC didn't have the time to decide if that was a compliment or not. All he knew was that he now had the situation completely under control and that was enough for his first assignment.

"You two," he called to the troublemakers as he held the back door of a large SUV open. "Step forward."

They complied and he patted them both down himself and

found no weapons. Pain tossed Agony a look and heard her murmur, "That's for me to know and for you to find out."

He chuckled and slid beside her in the back seat. Agent Simmons climbed in beside the driver and made it very clear to his passengers that he would not hesitate to put a bullet into each of their brains if they so much as sneezed in a way that displeased him.

Sergeant Jeffries entered his vehicle and took the mic as the officer behind the wheel pulled out.

"Sergeant Ishmael Jeffries," he reported to all channels. "Reported disturbance at parking garage is now under federal control. Three squads will provide backup to the federal agents until they reach their downtown headquarters and will then resume their scheduled rounds."

The report was greeted with ten-fours and the sergeant relaxed and enjoyed the ride because he had managed to piss on those who resided on the top of the hill. There might be hell to pay for it later but that wouldn't prevent him from enjoying the moment.

Harry T and his photographer watched the cavalcade head out.

"Shit, Harry," the photographer said, surprised that in all of the excitement, no one had tried to confiscate his cameras or discs. "You're onto something here."

The reporter nodded. "And that was only the first scratch on the surface, kiddo."

Pain and Agony knew that once they reached Fed Central, they would probably be separated, but thanks to her and her connections, at least one trustworthy officer in blue and one no-holds-barred member of the Fourth Estate were their backups for the moment.

"Doro disappears," Pain said as casually as if he were describing an episode of a TV show they'd both watched.

"Zaza meets a sidewalk." She laughed. "Dude, that must have hurt."

"Yeah, but after the commercial break, we learned that he bounced and toddled off."

"Who knew," she added cheerfully, "that he was practically indestructible?"

"Oh." Pain recounted the next episode. "And Doro made his way home. That one almost made me cry, I was so happy for him."

"What the fuck are you two talking about?" Agent Simmons asked. He wanted nothing more than for them to shut up while he tried to decide how to introduce them to his superiors and explain why he had taken them into custody.

"City-scape, Season One." Agony laughed. "You'd love it. Especially the one where the Budria goes boom-boom."

Pain elbowed her. "And Zaza says, I don't know no Budria Boom-Boom. Is she a stripper or something?"

The AiC shook his head and decided that whatever show they were talking about, he had no intention to ever watch it.

When they reached headquarters, the agent finally managed to separate them, visited the office of Special Agent TJ Varnes, and brought him up to date on the parking garage assignment.

"Are you telling me," Agent Varnes snapped, less than pleased, "that little Miss Agent Snitch slipped away quietly and left you with nothing to hold onto except your limp dick and two maybe suspects in an as yet unidentified operation?"

"Something like that, yes, sir." Simmons lowered his head as he waited for the rest of his ass to be chewed.

"And," Varnes continued, "the city boys in blue and a reporter were also on the scene?"

"I am afraid so. Someone had tipped them off."

The man sighed and shook his head. "Go get started on your

paperwork. The next time my sister asks me to do my nephew a favor, I'll tell her to tell him that maybe he isn't ready to move up through the ranks yet and a year or two heading up a field office in Omaha might do him good."

Agent Simmons backed out of the office, grateful to still have at least one butt cheek intact. All things considered, his Uncle TJ had gone lightly on him.

Left alone in his office and with the couple who had been brought in for questioning now secure in their individual rooms, Special Agent TJ Varnes took a moment to review the facts as he knew them.

Fact: His sister's kid had always been a bully and TJ had never been particularly fond of him. But when the boy had made a good showing at the Academy, he had pulled a few strings to have the kid assigned to his command where he could watch over and try to guide him.

Duncan had turned out to be a decent agent and he had to give the kid credit for not using his family connections to better himself. He had worked hard and had earned his first Agent in Charge assignment.

Fact: The young female agent from the Need to Know branch had thrown that division's weight around and forced the situation at the parking garage. At the first sign of it going south, she had disappeared.

Fact: He now had two citizens in his custody with both the police and the press aware of it.

It was time for him to personally put out whatever fire was now burning, even if it meant chugging a gallon of water and pissing on any flames he could find. He turned to his computer and put in all the data he had at his disposal. Having studied and printed it out, he put the files in two separate folders and decided to tackle the ex-cop first.

"Goni, first name Alicia." Varnes tossed the folder onto the table, sat across from her, and leaned forward.

"Oh, good." She leaned back. "You know how to read. But if your eyes get tired, I can save you the trouble of reading the whole file and tell you how the story ends."

"I managed to finish the file all by myself, thank you for the offer." He softened his tone but didn't lean back. "Orders came from above that we were to pick you up and bring you in."

"Those are certainly interesting orders." She also softened her tone but didn't lean forward. "Where are the order issuers now and why aren't they questioning me?"

"I have no idea." He stated the truth with a shrug. "You are free to go."

"That's it?" She was mock-skeptical. "No thumbscrews?"

"You know as well as I do," the agent continued and reminded himself of the truth as he knew it to be, "that there is at least one city policeman who is still on your side and will wait to make sure you walk out of here. Oh, and a reporter." He sighed. "I could deal with one or the other but I have no intention to try to fight them both, especially for reasons that I have not yet been given. Have a nice life."

He picked the file up and moved to the door.

"And the man I was brought in with?" she asked as the agent placed his hand on the doorknob.

"Oh, him," Varnes turned and answered. "I am about to have a chat with him now." He tapped the other folder he was holding. "It should be a very interesting interview, especially given the fact that he doesn't exist."

With that parting shot, he walked out and left the door open behind him.

Another fed came into the room.

"You are," he informed her, "free to go. I am simply here as an escort whose assignment is to make sure you find your way out without any side trips along the way."

Agony rose and followed him until they reached the front doors. She stepped onto the plaza of Fed Central and sat on a bench with her gaze fixed on the front door while she waited.

"First name initial, M." The fed tossed a folder down on the table in front of Pain. "Last name initial, P. I am Special Agent TJ Varnes. Please help me to get through this interview as quickly as possible so I can return to burying my head under a stack of paperwork in the hope that I can suffocate myself to death."

"Agent TJ Varnes." The big man leaned back in his chair as if he didn't have a care in the world. "You have nothing, do you?"

He opened the folder that held one sheet of paper in it. "You have that right, Mister Whoever the Fuck you Really Are."

"Oh good." The man leaned forward. "That admission will save us both considerable time. Whoever I am, I have no recorded history of violence or criminal record at all. For all intents and purposes, I am merely an innocent schmuck you pulled in off the street to practice your rubber-hose routine on. That makes you seem like the bad guys now, doesn't it?"

"It does not present us in a very good light," the agent admitted.

"And here is some more light." The man's voice turned as hard as his eyes. "Your superiors are under the impression that Uncle Sam taught me how to be the baddest-assed sum'bitch on the planet but that is all horse shit. I learned how to be that man all on my own. But what my time under Uncle Sam's tutelage did teach me was that every assignment had a paper trail filled out in triplicate to either be shredded if a job went bad, or filed somewhere for future reference if a job went well. I developed my own filing system. There are only three people on this earth who know how to access it and none of their names will appear in any file."

"And what," Special Agent TJ Varnes asked, "do you want me to do now that you've shared that information with me?"

"I want you to save the recording of this conversation and watch me stand and walk out into the sunshine. They can bury my body but they can't bury the truth. Too many people have access to it."

Varnes remained silent as the big man stood and sauntered toward the door, where he paused and turned to look at him for one last word.

"He has your eyes."

"Who?" He had not expected to hear that as a final salvo.

"The boy in the parking garage. He has your eyes."

Fuck all to hell. This bastard doesn't miss a thing.

"Actually," he conceded, "he has my sister's eyes."

"Stay righteous," were the last words the man who didn't exist said before he turned and walked casually away.

"So, did you miss me?" Pain asked as he walked into the sunshine to where Agony waited for him.

"We need to make sure Bertha hasn't been completely stripped of all of her parts by now."

"Who is this we that you speak of?" he asked.

"The Psycho Commando and the Butch Bitch, of course," she answered as she wrapped an arm around his elbow and they strolled to the street to hail a cab. "I hear that they make one helluva team."

"Well, one of the team is starving. Can we at least stop for a pizza along the way?"

"No, no, no." She flagged down a cab. "I won't have any appetite until I learn that Bertha is safe."

"That doesn't mean I'm not starving for a pizza." He truly was hungry.

"Compromise time," she suggested. "Bertha first. Bibimbap pizza second?"

He held the back door of the cab open as she slid in first. He followed and gave the driver the address to the Imperial Palace where Bertha, a bibimbap pizza, and two cots could be found.

The story continues with book 2, *Cry Havoc*, coming soon to Amazon and to Kindle Unlimited.

CREATOR NOTES
SEPTEMBER 8, 2021

First, thank you for not only reading this story but these author notes in the back as well.

For those who don't know me, I'll put a "Who am I?" in just a second. For those who do, I'll give you a quick update. I am presently in northern Nevada on the I-15 heading north toward Provo, UT. The person driving with me is author Craig Martelle, a best friend and my co-author on many collaborations in science fiction.

This idea of driving across America was Craig's. I suspect the fifteen-day trip (I'm along for five days) was his effort to get the hell out of Alaska. The leaves are turning and falling off the trees, and the temperatures are getting ready to plummet where he lives in the North Pole area.

Craig is escaping; I know it.

I don't blame him, but I've been roped into his trek across America, where each night we stop and have dinner with authors.

Next book, I'll try to remember to tell you about how I came up with the *Pain and Agony* characters while heading out to eat pizza one night.

Ok, now a little about me if you haven't met me.

I wrote my first book *Death Becomes Her* (*The Kurtherian Gambit*) in September/October of 2015 and released it November 2, 2015. I wrote and released the next two books that same month and had three released by the end of November 2015.

So, just under six years ago.

Since then, I've written, collaborated, concepted, and/or created hundreds more in all sorts of genres.

My most successful genre is still my first, Paranormal Sci-Fi, followed quickly by Urban Fantasy. I have multiple pen names I produce under.

Some because I can be a bit crude in my humor at times or raw in my cynicism (Michael Todd). I have one I share with Martha Carr (Judith Berens, and another (not disclosed) that we use as a marketing test pen name.

In general, I just love to tell stories, and with success comes the opportunity to mix two things I love in my life.

Business and stories.

I've wanted to be an entrepreneur since I was a teenager. I was a very *unsuccessful* entrepreneur (I tried many times) until my publishing company LMBPN signed one author in 2015.

Me.

I was the president of the company, and I was the first author published. Funny how it worked out that way.

It was late 2016 before we had additional authors join me for publishing. Now we have a few dozen authors, a few hundred audiobooks by LMBPN published, a few hundred more licensed by six audio companies, and about a thousand titles in our company.

It's been a busy five plus years.

Ad Aeternitatem,
Michael Anderle

BOOKS BY MICHAEL ANDERLE

Sign up for the LMBPN email list to be notified of new releases and special deals!

https://lmbpn.com/email/

For a complete list of books by Michael Anderle, please visit:

www.lmbpn.com/ma-books/

CONNECT WITH MICHAEL

Connect with Michael Anderle

Website: http://lmbpn.com

Email List: http://lmbpn.com/email/

https://www.facebook.com/LMBPNPublishing

https://twitter.com/MichaelAnderle

https://www.instagram.com/lmbpn_publishing/

https://www.bookbub.com/authors/michael-anderle

Made in United States
Orlando, FL
23 January 2022

13944922R00146